KEEPERS OF THE MARSH

Maura Jortner

HOLIDAY HOUSE · NEW YORK

To all the fraternal twins out there

Copyright © 2025 by Maura Jortner
All Rights Reserved
HOLIDAY HOUSE is registered in the U.S. Patent and Trademark Office.
Printed and bound in March 2025 at Sheridan, Chelsea, MI, USA.
www.holidayhouse.com
First Edition
1 3 5 7 9 10 8 6 4 2

Library of Congress Cataloging-in-Publication Data is available.

ISBN: 978-0-8234-5791-5 (hardcover)

EU Authorized Representative: HackettFlynn Ltd, 36 Cloch Choirneal,
Balrothery, Co. Dublin, K32 C942, Ireland.
EU@walkerpublishinggroup.com

"The Alligator Witch"

When the weather turns bad,
And when the rain clings,
The Witch comes around
Prowling for live things—

You'll see her in the waves,
In the wind the storm brings,
The Alligator Witch
Prowling for live things—

You can hear the warning bells
And she's in every ding,
The Alligator Witch
Prowling for live things—

So shut tight your doors,
Tie them down with strings
When the Witch comes around
Prowling for live things—

No one can be safe,
Not even queens or kings,
From the Alligator Witch
Prowling for live things

—Song sung in Galveston, Texas

Chapter One

There's a witch that lives in the marsh by West Bay. They say her house lies in the stand of trees, where the marsh is the muddiest and the weeds are tall and tangly.

No one knows how she got there. *Leave her alone*, say the people around town. *She's a mean one—she must be*, they speculate.

I should be scared.

Sometimes, though, I dream about her.

Chapter Two

It was the point in summer when I had watched every video on the internet, listened to all the music that ever existed, beat every free game I could access on my phone, and spent as much time outside as any twelve-year-old could stomach.

Yeah: it was early August. School was starting soon, and I was actually looking forward to classes beginning because I was Bored with a capital *B*. Bored beyond Bored. I was Bored enough to try to take a nap to help the time pass.

Hint: I didn't fall asleep.

I lay in bed, still awake, with Tofu, my cat, draped across my feet. Ever since we got him, he has weighed more than any cat should. He is what my little sister (lovingly) called a "Big Boy." When he settles down on you, you know it.

"Hey, Tofu buddy," I said—and yes, I said this out loud. I talked to my cat, what of it? I figured as long as I didn't expect him to answer, it was fine. "Do you think it's time to get off me?" I asked. "Should we move from the bed?" I shifted the top half of my body so I could see him. Brown-gray with black tiger stripes. Curled up. His fluffy kitty head resting on his soft kitty paws. He opened one eye to look at me but closed it again as if to say *No thanks, I'm fine staying.* "You might be snoozing, but this girl is wide awake." I pointed to myself in case he was unsure.

He squeezed his eyes shut tighter and snuggled down more like he wanted to prove to me how comfy he was.

My twin sister's music turned on and drifted through the wall.

Since her bedroom was next to mine, I got the firsthand earful of what she was up to. From the beat and the singer's high voice, I could tell: it was K-pop. Then again, it was always K-pop. That girl loved K-pop.

I would have rather listened to anything else, but that was how it was with me and Gracie—we might have been twins, we might have spent nine months in the womb together, but we didn't understand each other.

Fraternal twins, but still.

Bump, bump, bump. Ba-bump. Ba-bump. Ba-bump.

People who ate spinach and broccoli and asparagus on purpose—they made more sense to me than Gracie.

"Okay, Tofu," I said with more umph. "I know you're enjoying your nap, but we should go." I knew from past experience that once Gracie started listening to K-pop, she'd be at it for hours. Staying in bed with that kind of knock-yourself-out drumbeat and a crooning voice—cat snuggled up on me or not—wasn't my idea of a good time. I scooted my left foot out from under him.

He opened his eyes and blinked at me like he was offended. I swear, I could see a kitty frown forming on his little kitty mouth.

"Sorry, buddy," I said, "but the music, you know?"

He didn't. He would be happy to snooze on me all day long, annoying music or not. But for me, enough was enough. As I pulled my right foot toward my body, he made a noise, something between a meow of displeasure and a yawn.

"I love you, buddy," I said. "You know that." His cat belly was firmly on the bed, not resting on me anymore, and maybe to protest that fact, he rose and stretched, Halloween-cat style. He leaped off, landed on the rug, and strutted toward the door without so much as a glance back.

"Thanks, Tofu. I mean it."

His bottom swayed side to side, and he held his tail in the air in the shape of a question mark.

"I love you," I said again, because I did, even if I wasn't up for spending the day with his heavy cat-self resting on my feet while the sounds of K-pop wafted through the wall. I swung my legs down. One foot had fallen asleep, so I let it tingle and hum before placing it gingerly onto the floor and limping from the room.

Gracie's music was louder in the hall. She wore headphones, so I shouldn't have been able to hear it. If it was set to a normal, not blow-out-your-eardrums level, I would have only heard the soft *whir* of the AC. Or perhaps Tofu's paws padding across the living room floor. Or maybe the *buzz* of the refrigerator. Instead, her music came through loud and clear.

Was I going to do something about this? Heck no. They were her eardrums. Her problem. Besides, I had stuff to do. A mission to accomplish. I was going to ask Mom to take us somewhere. I'd struck out on this all summer, but I hoped if I asked her super-duper nicely, things would change. She would say yes, and I would find a way out of this boring, do-nothing day. Okay, realistically, I didn't think I had a shot in H-E-double-hockey-sticks of getting Mom to do anything, but it was worth a try. A kid's got to try.

Mom and Duck were in the living room, sitting on the couch. Seeing them so close together brought out how alike they were. It was like looking at a person and her miniature.

But it wasn't just Duck. All the females in my family looked the same.

Mom, Gracie, and Duck had perfect dark brown hair that formed perfect ringlets that danced around their perfect heads. They had perfect small shoulders and perfect small frames.

I was the one who was out of place.

Orange-brown hair. Short. Stocky build. Blue eyes.

No, not entirely out of place. I looked like Dad.

That was fine with me. I wanted to be like him. He was amazing—a great person.

Was.

Still, I wished I looked more like Mom and my sisters now and then. I was the "ugly twin" to the kids at school. The one that airport security guards eyed when we were all together. I was the one who'd been asked if she was adopted. I was the square peg that didn't fit into the round hole.

Crumbs.

Mom had earbuds in and that faraway look she got when she was listening to an audio book. Duck held her Nintendo Switch like she was gripping on for life itself. Her knuckles were white, and she was moving her shoulders back and forth in a chaotic way that had to mean she was in an epic fight or battle or doing some really wild, amazing driving.

"Die, die, die!" she said through gritted teeth.

A battle, then.

I wasn't a fan of the word *die* anymore. Not since Dad passed away two years ago. Then again, that's the difference between real life and video games. Online, death was temporary. You died, you got to spawn back in the next minute. Death in reality was something else—permanent, heartbreaking, forever.

Maybe that's why Duck liked video games so much.

I settled onto the couch near her and leaned over to see, but she swung that Switch so hard and fast, I couldn't make out a thing.

"Is that Minecraft?" I asked.

"Bunch of endermen." She kept punching the buttons, so the mob must not have been letting up.

"Good luck," I said. Then I lowered my voice. "Hey, I was thinking about asking Mom to bring us somewhere." Mom was sitting on the other side of the couch, but I didn't think she'd hear me over the audio book if I kept it down.

"Gotta fight," Duck said.

I held back the urge to roll my eyes. I remembered being ten years old. All I wanted to do was play on my Switch too.

Duck's real name is Doucette. Mom's side of the family is French American. In point of fact: Mom's name is Amelie. But Dad was—how would he put it? He didn't have an exciting background. His family had been in America for centuries. His name was Chad. So Gracie and I got names in that fashion. Lana and Gracie. Nothing cool like Doucette or Amelie.

At least our names didn't rhyme. I didn't think I could forgive my parents if they had gone that way. So many twins got abominable names that came in pairs—Tara and Sara, Chloe and Zoe, Laura and Nora. No, thank you. That would have been worse than poison, worse than burning at the stake, worse than having to listen to K-pop all day.

Lana meant *calm as still waters*, which was nothing like me.

Gracie—well, that was nothing like her either.

"You don't want to go to the beach?" I asked Duck, still keeping my voice low.

"I'm at a good part," she whined back to me.

"It's Minecraft," I said. "It goes on forever, and you could always start a new game."

Duck didn't answer, only scrunched up her lips. She wasn't going to help.

"You could bring it with you," I said, meaning the Switch.

She squeezed her lips into a thin line and gave me a look. "Sand," she said, as if it was obvious. "The controller could get ruined, and Mom said if I break another one, that's it."

"Mom didn't mean it," I said.

In return, she stared at me—quick but deadly—before continuing on with that battle.

"Okay, I get it," I said, but it wasn't true. Mom might give Duck a hard time about getting another set of Joy-Cons, but trust me, she would have. Duck got what Duck wanted. As the baby of the family, she was treated like the Parker Family Unicorn—special privileges, a later bedtime than Gracie or I ever had at that age, extended time to play video games. Duck was pampered.

So, the fear of no Switch for a day or two wasn't what was keeping her from helping me convince Mom to bring us somewhere. No, Duck was like Mom now, too ready to find an excuse to stay home.

We'd been doing this—this whole bunch of nothing—since Dad died. He used to take us everywhere. The beach, the zoo in Houston, museums, Moody Gardens, the amusement park on the pier ... everywhere. Our family had plans every weekend. He'd turn to us while we were eating dinner on Friday night and say, "Where should we go this weekend?" Gracie and I would spout off possibilities in rapid fire and he'd nod along, saying, "Maybe, maybe," and finally he'd get a big smile on his face and sing, *Daht, dah, dah, daaa!*" and he'd turn his phone around so we could see the screen and there would be a picture of the place we were off to. Every weekend. It was amazing.

We hadn't left the house other than to go to the grocery store, school, or the doctor since then. Two years.

It was time for a change.

And I was just bored enough to make it happen.

"If I convince her," I said to Duck, "I'll get you a Ziploc bag so you can keep your Switch safe, okay?" I reached over to ruffle her perfect curly dark hair, but she pulled her head away.

She grunted a sound of displeasure.

I didn't let it bother me.

I moved to Mom's side of the couch and pointed at my ears and mouthed a bunch of nonsense, not making any sound but pretending to, until she realized I wanted her to stop listening to that dang book. My bet? It was one of those self-help, inspirational things. She listened to them all the time since Dad died.

Mom was an English teacher, and she wore dorky English teacher shirts. Today's said, **HYPERBOLE: THE MOST AMAZING AND EXTRAORDINARY WORD IN THE HISTORY OF LANGUAGE.** Funny... kind of. If you went in for that type of thing. She was like that—dorky with a sense of humor. Or she used to be. She hadn't bought a new shirt for the last two years either.

She slipped off her earbuds.

"Hey, Mom, um, so, I was thinking about all the great times we used to have and all the fun before so how about we head to the beach?" I sped through the question as if she might nod and agree before she realized what she was doing.

Instead, she frowned and said, "The beach?" She sounded like she'd never heard of it. Like we didn't live fifteen minutes from the coast. As if we weren't on an island with a long stretch of perfect sand and water.

"We haven't been in forever," I said.

Mom leaned back against the couch cushion hard, in a way that signaled unease. "It's so hot, Lana."

I plucked my phone from my back pocket and hit the weather app. A high of 93. That, plus the humidity, meant she was right. But I wasn't giving up.

"We're tough," I said.

"And those tourists." Mom said the word *tourists* like they were the worst people in the world.

Okay, she had a point on that too. Tourists were the worst, and Galveston, Texas, got plenty of them, even now, in the dog days of summer.

"But...," I said, and my voice came out too high, so I cleared my throat and adjusted it before going on, "but we haven't been anywhere in so long and I'm so bored."

Mom raised a finger, and I knew what was coming. I could have said the words along with her: "Only boring people get bored."

I pinched the bridge of my nose. "I'm not sure that's true, Mom."

"A great philosopher once said it."

She had told me that before too but could never seem to come up with this wise philosopher's actual name.

I needed to shift gears.

"How about Moody Gardens? It's indoors, so we won't sweat our brains out. Remember when Dad took us? Gosh, it was a long time ago. We saw fish and penguins and birds. I think there was a movie too."

"Die, die, die!" Duck said.

I pretended that she'd said something else—maybe "I remember that!" or, "Yeah, let's go!"

"It was fun, right?" I said to my little sister.

"Ugh," Mom grunted. "It'll be so crowded. How about we go in September when it's just the locals?"

Her suggestion wasn't a bad one, but if I knew Mom—and I did—she wasn't going to take us on a family trip to Moody Gardens in September either. School would be back in session and that meant she'd have homework and grading and driving us back and forth and dinners to make and cleaning to do ... and I got it. Being a single parent was a nightmare. She was a mess from late August until mid-May, and then she got some precious time to relax.

Unfortunately, that meant we were stuck at home doing nothing.

What made the situation worse was that my best friends, Julianna and Kaylee, were out of town, unreachable. Julianna was at a sleepaway camp for Girl Scouts and Kaylee was on vacation with her family. The Girl Scouts didn't allow phones, and Kaylee was in Disney World—too busy having a grand old time to FaceTime or send more than a few pictures my way. So it was just me, with my boring family, doing nothing, nothing, nothing.

This was it. I had to convince Mom. I made a sad face. "Please, Mom? Please, please, please?" Was I begging? You betcha. It had come to that.

Mom gave a loud sigh and slipped an earbud back in. "We'll see, okay?"

That meant no.

The other earbud went in and that was that. Conversation over.

I was doomed to suffer more Boredom with a capital *B*.

Chapter Three

I thought if I had to look at the inside of my house one second longer, I might do something drastic—climb a bookcase or attempt to squish myself under the couch or see if I could gnaw through a chair leg using only my teeth.

In other words, I needed a change in location, pronto.

And there was one place I could go. One place always open to me.

"I'll be at Nana's," I said to Duck, since Mom wasn't listening anymore.

"It's raining on my garden in Minecraft," she said. "How weird is that?"

Nana had lived next door to us for as long as I'd been alive. She had a stroke in March, and so she had to move into a nursing home near downtown. Stoney Brook Care Center. It was a nice place. Not too far. Maybe twenty minutes by car. I hadn't been to see her in a while. None of us had—part of our stay-at-home-all-the-time routine.

Her house, on the other hand, was right next door and it could be my getaway destination.

I gave Duck a wave when I reached the door. She didn't look up from her Switch. Mom leaned back on the couch as if transported to another world. Well, I hoped she was having a good time there. Me, I was still bored in this world.

But Nana's would help.

By the time I was down the porch steps and up Nana's, I was sweating like every gland in my body was trying to produce its own river. Yup, Galveston in August. Even at 10:30 in the morning it was a sweat-fest.

Nana kept a key hidden on the top of a window ledge. It was up high and out of view, hard to find unless you knew it was there. I was on the short side, so I had to pull off a major stretch to reach it. After elongating my body in the hopes of making it a few inches taller than nature intended, I got a fingertip on it and slid it down and opened the door.

Nana's house was almost empty. Seeing it stripped to the bare bones made me suck in a breath. Every time. It was so different from when she'd been here, from when life had been normal, that it still affected me, made my lungs feel tight. Only some furniture remained and a few of her things. Most everything else had gone with her to the nursing home, and then the rest had been put into storage.

Stoney Brook Care Center was one of those places where you could live for many years, so Mom had moved Nana in, thinking she could recover from the stroke, then settle in and make friends. Be happy and well taken care of.

Nana had other ideas.

A few months ago, Nana made it clear to Mom that she was NOT staying in the nursing home permanently—all capital letters. Nana couldn't talk anymore because of the stroke, so this communication happened in writing. Can you imagine that interaction? Here's how it played out in my mind:

Mom said, "Clem, this place is great. You should stay put."

Nana wrote on a piece of paper: *I'M COMING HOME ASAP!!!*

Mom said, "Just think about it, okay? Having a whole house to take care of is a lot. And you might want to rest more."

Nana pointed at the writing.

Mom: "Just think about it. I'm trying to be considerate, Clem."

Nana pointed at the writing.

Mom: "Just—"

Nana pointed again.

That was Nana for you. Opinionated as a wet cat.

Despite her insistence, I wasn't sure she would be returning home. The last time I saw her, she was using a walker, and I didn't know how she expected to climb up all those stairs to reach her front porch with a walker.

I closed the door behind me and took a few steps toward the shelving unit, which was built into the far wall.

Even without Nana here, her house was a great place to hang out. No annoying sister with loud music. No other sister shouting, "*Die!*" No Mom staring off into space. And at least I could be surrounded by a different set of walls.

No one had packed up the collection of board games, and I eyed Nana's selection. Playing a board game by yourself wasn't the greatest, I'll be the first to admit it, but if you used your imagination, it could work. I grabbed the Game of Life because it was fun to set up and I figured I could make a few different choices along the way to see which game decisions were most successful. You could almost say I was doing research, research for future Friday nights—future "Family Fun Time"... if Nana was right about returning home.

Nana established Family Fun Time after Dad died. Cheesy, sure, but she was close to seventy, so we didn't argue with her about it.

She showed up one Friday evening, after a super-duper long school week, and told us to get over to her house ASAP. When we arrived, the smell of pizza made our mouths water. She'd gotten takeout from our favorite place—Mama Theresa's Flying Pizza. Even better, there were three different kinds of soda. Everyone could have the one they liked. With a wink, she told Mom to go home, take the night off. She had this.

After Mom left, we dug into that food and Nana selected a game for us—Yahtzee. She'd dug it out of her closet, a forgotten relic of the past. We hadn't played before and it seemed suspiciously like doing math with dice, but it was fun. We played and played until we were so tired, we couldn't tell if we had a small straight or a full house or just three of a kind, and we ate so much pizza and downed so much soda, our bellies hurt. Gracie slept on the pull-out couch. I snuggled up on the big armchair. Nana and Duck shared her bed in the bedroom.

Nana did some serious online shopping after that, and her living room shelves filled up with all kinds of games. Sure, there were the ones that existed eons ago and she knew how to play—Monopoly and Twister and the Game of Life. But she bought newer ones too—Poetry for Neanderthals, One Night Ultimate Werewolf, Exploding Kittens. When I asked her how she picked them, she told me that she watched YouTube videos. If the game didn't look too hard, she'd purchase it right away.

That was Nana.

Was.

Family Fun Time got better and better every week.

Until March.

Since then, everything had felt hopeless. It was just us and Mom and, once summertime hit, boredom.

I toted the Game of Life to the kitchen table because that's where Family Fun Time used to happen, and I wanted to feel like I was playing with more people than yours truly. The kitchen was empty, other than the table and chairs. I went to the fridge and looked inside, just in case. Nope. Stark and white. I opened cabinets, hoping for a snack. Nothing. It was like that nursery rhyme where the lady looks for a bone for her dog and finds none.

Oh well. I'd get a little hungry, maybe, but it was better than enduring K-pop. I got down to setting up the game and it was as satisfying as I remembered. I loved clicking in the hills and the bridges and the white buildings. I sorted the money and got out four cars and started spinning that dial, which never worked as well as it should but made your heart dance anyway.

The first car—yellow—was a man and woman with five kids and two lousy-paying jobs. The blue man-peg drove. Very traditional types. They were poor, but happy, and at the end of the game they chose to go to Countryside Acres. A smart choice.

The second car—red—was a lesbian couple that had a baby girl. They earned a ton of money. They were happy for different reasons, and as I moved their car along the road, I hopped it up and down to show how gleeful they were. They ended up in Millionaire Estates and won the game.

The third car—green—was middle of the road money-wise. A teacher's pay and two kids. When I spun a ten, the mom (pink lady-peg) complained to the dad (blue man-peg) that he was driving too fast.

My own sense of humor.

They did pretty well and went to Millionaire Estates even though it was clear they didn't have as much money as the red car. Maybe hubris got them in the end. They ended up being second.

The fourth car—blue—was a family with really bad luck.

They landed on every Pay Taxes spot. They got in car accidents. People sued them. They were victims of fraud. They almost went bankrupt three times. When they ended the game, a sole pink twenty-thousand-dollar bill sat in front of their spot on the table. Countryside Acres was the only option.

I was considering starting another round when my phone buzzed with a text.

Where are you?

It was Mom.

Nana's, I texted back. Great. Duck hadn't told her—that was so Duck. Then again, when I said to Duck that I was headed to Nana's, she'd replied by telling me it was raining in her game. I, like everyone else, became white noise when she was playing. *I told Duck where I was going*, I texted. I didn't want Mom thinking I'd left without a word.

Come back by lunch, she answered.

I sent a thumbs-up.

It was almost noon, so I didn't have enough time for another game. I packed up the bridges and buildings. I tucked the spinner and the board game into the box.

Now what?

After putting the game back on the shelf, I found myself wandering into Nana's room, the primary bedroom. Her bed was gone. Now, there were only marks on the rug where it used to stand. Her closet was empty too. The only thing left was a bureau that I guessed was too big for her room at Stoney Brook. I rubbed my hand across its top. Some kind of longing filled my insides. Longing for how things were before.

I missed Nana. She was the leader of our family. The one who kept us from falling apart after Dad was gone.

Was.

Now she was gone too, or at least not next door, and everything was different.

Everything had changed.

I opened the drawers of the bureau, one by one. Empty, empty, empty. Until I came to the bottom right. Seeing what was inside made me gasp. It was Dad's stuff. Whoa. I hadn't set eyes on it for years.

I went through his things: His favorite book (a Carl Hiaasen novel). An academic work on the Industrial Revolution (tedious). His University of Houston polo. (He wore it everywhere.) His wallet (full). I flipped it open to get a look at his license, his picture. It was a terrible photo that didn't look like him, or not how I remembered him, anyway.

There was something else at the back of the drawer. The corner of something white. I tugged on it, but it wouldn't budge. I tugged harder. The crack of the drawer held on to it, like whatever it was had been there forever.

This would require some muscles.

I put my back into it.

When it pulled free, I was holding an envelope. White and ordinary. Pretty boring... except for what was written on it: *Important—Chad.*

Chapter Four

I had a choice. I could open it or not. It was addressed to Dad, so if I did look inside, I would be reading something that wasn't meant for me. I might even be breaking the law. But here was the thing: Dad wasn't coming back. Dad would never open it himself. It was me or no one, and this seemed important. Heck, the word *important* was written right on the front.

Dad had died of a virus. It was that simple—a stupid virus. We all had it. The rest of the family got better; he got worse. When he told Mom he felt like he couldn't breathe, she said, "Let's get you to the hospital. I'll drive." She grabbed her keys. They jingled in her hand.

Dad shook his head and wheezed out, "The kids."

Gracie and I had just turned ten. Duck was eight. It was early morning in the middle of the summer, and we were still in our pj's. We hadn't even had breakfast yet.

Mom looked pained. "We could ask Clem to bring you."

Clem—Nana.

"No," Dad said softly, shaking his head. He braced himself on the chair like he didn't have the energy to stand. "I'll get there."

"Clem could come here," Mom argued, "and I could go with you."

"Germs," Dad said.

He didn't want Nana to get sick. She hadn't caught it yet.

So it was decided. Mom gave him a nod and that was that.

Off he went, alone. We didn't even hug him goodbye. We didn't know what would come next.

He was admitted to the hospital later that day and then moved to the ICU. He died a week later.

And then he was just... gone.

In the days afterward, a hole opened in my chest and filled with cold, swirling water. It made me feel like I was drowning. He'd said he felt like he couldn't breathe, and I felt that way too, but for a different reason.

The hole was mostly filled in now. Over months and months, earth had packed in, hard and tight. But every now and then—like, let's say, when I found an envelope with his name on it—the hole opened again and that water swished around, splashing into every crevice of my insides.

It sprayed up and filled my eyes with tears.

"Dad...," I whispered.

Should I open the envelope? It wasn't meant for me.

But I couldn't leave it. I just couldn't. It would be like leaving a piece of Dad behind.

I stretched out my hand, a dress rehearsal of sorts, and placed the envelope back in the drawer. I closed the drawer, stood, turned around. My hands trembled and I braced myself on the bureau. That hole in my insides got deeper, and the water became a torrent. Nope, I wasn't going to walk away.

I whipped that drawer open, grabbed the envelope, and tore it open.

Inside I found a golden key attached to a blue ribbon. "Huh," I said as I pulled it out and let it hang down. The ribbon was long and tied in a loop, like you could hang it on a hook.

There was also a note. It was worn around the edges, and fancy, cursive writing—like the kind on the front of the envelope—said, *Do your duty. The Alligator Witch is always there.*

"The Alligator Witch," I whispered.

My phone buzzed.

Time for lunch. Mom again.

Did I take it with me or leave it there?

The choice was easy. I'd already opened it, after all.

I shoved the note and the key with the soft ribbon back in the envelope and tucked the whole shebang in my back pocket.

Duck was skipping toward Nana's house as I shut the front door and locked it before reaching up, up to get that key back in its hiding place.

"I'm coming," I called to her.

"Okay," she called back. She skipped away in the opposite direction. Mom must have sent her to get me.

I trudged down the long set of stairs, my mind feeling heavy and slow moving.

What did the note mean? What did Dad have to do with the Alligator Witch? The writing implied he was supposed to do something—a duty. Something with that key, and something that had to do with her, the witch. But wasn't she just a town legend?

In our yard, I stopped to look at the marsh, which sat behind our house. It stretched out far in both directions. To the left, it went past Nana and the LaSalles' house, past the palm trees along the quiet road, all the way to where the street curved. To the right, it journeyed past the cul de sac and kept going as far as the eye could see, out until the bay took over. The grass in my yard was scorched and crunchy—brown after enduring months of the hot Texas summer.

The marsh was another story. I can tell it to you in one word: muddy. In the spring, it became a myriad of stars when the sunlight hit the pools of water, and if you squinted, it was like looking at a hidden, wet palace of endless starlight. But during summer it was mostly just brown and gooey. The grass that grew near the small pools of water was tall, bent over in the hot breeze. There were prickly plants and flowers and scraggly little bushes. Most of everything was under a foot tall. Everything except for one stand of trees off to the left—the one thing for miles that stood high and always seemed to be in a shadow. That was where the Alligator Witch lived. Supposedly.

Was she real?

No one knew for sure.

At some point, way back, my family had put up an electric fence to make sure no one went into the marsh by accident. My great-grandfather maybe. He wanted to stop someone with a shock before they reached the real danger.

Breeze blew against me, which was nice—refreshing—until the smell kicked in. French fries. It must have been coming from Waterman's Restaurant, which was on the road that led to the beach. Don't get me wrong: I like French fries. I adore them. But when you can only *smell* them, it feels like a tragedy. More than any kid should have to bear. It made me want to run inside and gobble up whatever Mom had made for lunch... but I stayed there, eyeing that stand of trees.

Duck kept skipping in small circles. She wiped sweat off her upper lip and came my way. "Whatcha looking at?"

"The Alligator Witch's house."

She stopped next to me and held her hand over her eyes, blocking out the sun's rays, to peer across the mud and grass and standing water. "She's not real."

"She might be real," I said. I could feel that envelope in my back pocket. A key and a note inside about the witch. A duty.

"Nah," Duck said.

"Dad believed in her."

"So does Nana."

"So she might be real," I said, triumph making my voice strong. "That's two adults, and adults we trust."

Trusted, I amended in my head. I didn't say that part out loud.

"Maybe." Duck shrugged and skipped away toward our house, singing the song all kids her age sang:

"Alligator Witch in the marshy trees.
Nasty, nasty mean old witch is she.
Die, witchy-witchy, die, witchy-witchy.
Please just let us be."

Duck zoomed up our stairs and pushed the front door open, but slowly. "Tofu's in the way," she said when I joined her on the porch.

Like most cats, Tofu's main purpose in life seemed to be to remind you of his existence and to possibly annoy you while doing so. Finally, Duck got the door open, and we stepped inside in time to see him run off like we had startled him. Like we were to blame. I rolled my eyes so far back I might have seen the inside of my skull. I mean, you'd think he'd learn his lesson about sitting in front of the door by now, but no. Cats, am I right?

Mom backed against the wall to make room for him as he scurried past her. "Oh, good, you're home," she said to us.

"What's for lunch?" Duck asked.

"Mac and cheese," Mom said.

"My favorite," Duck said.

That's why Mom made it. She made it most days. She made it so often I thought I might develop lactose intolerance.

"Thanks, Mom," Duck said, and she ran over to Mom, who gave her a side hug. Like I said, Parker Family Unicorn.

———•———

Lunchtime. Mom let us eat in front of the TV. I gave myself an internal pep talk on my way to the armchair, where I normally sat: *You can do this. You can get along with Gracie for a half hour.*

Sure, that's what I told myself, but I wasn't certain I could. I needed a degree in statistics to figure out the actual probability, but let's say it was close to fifty-fifty. Fifty percent chance I could hold myself together. Fifty percent chance I'd lose it. Gracie did that to me.

I took my seat. Gracie and Duck sat on the couch as Mom passed out bowls of mac and cheese. Gracie had the remote (crumbs!) and she clicked on YouTube and started scrolling. She was on her profile, headed for the recently watched.

"Not a K-drama," I said with a moan.

"Why not?" She shot me a look.

"Because those shows are boring."

"No they're not."

"Please don't argue," Mom said as she returned to the kitchen.

"No one likes them but you," I said to Gracie.

K-dramas were all about love and romance. Gracie's favorite—*Linked-In*—followed couples (or soon-to-be couples), filming them talking about the other person and saying what they liked about them. Gracie thought it was the sweetest thing in the world. I thought it was either irritating or creepy, depending on the couple.

"I vote for Disney," Duck said, mouth already full of mac and cheese.

"I'll tell you who the couples are," Gracie said. She was scrolling down through the videos, in season sixteen, or something like that. "I'll give you their backstories."

"No way," I spouted. "Find something we all like."

"But this one is so good," Gracie pleaded.

Hint: it was not going to be so good.

"How about a superhero movie?" I suggested. "There are plenty on Netflix."

"Too violent," Gracie said. She looked scared already.

"But the new Spider-Man one is a cartoon. That won't be bad."

"People die in it," Gracie said, "and I heard there are jump scares."

"*Pretend* people," I said, emphasis on *pretend*. "They're animated."

"Can't we watch something *regular*?" Gracie asked, and I swear there may have been tears in her voice.

I did not understand that girl. Crying over a TV show? At the suggestion of a superhero movie? During *lunch*? During a lunch of fake cheese and processed starch?

"Whatever," I said, and I shoved a huge bite in my mouth so I could be done with this sooner rather than later.

"Dis-ney, Dis-ney, Dis-ney!" Duck chanted.

In the end, Gracie put on a movie about a princess, which I watched for about twenty minutes. I thought it was a good display of patience on my part.

The entire time I was eating, though, I was thinking about that envelope, which was still in my back pocket. When I got into my room, I tugged it out.

The key. The ribbon. The strange note. What did it mean?

Do your duty. The Alligator Witch is always there.

It sounded to me like Dad had something to do before he died. Something he was supposed to accomplish.

But maybe he hadn't done it.

Chapter Five

By late afternoon, I couldn't hold in my curiosity any longer. I decided I was going to ask Mom about the Alligator Witch. It was a bad idea, but I couldn't stop myself. She was the only person around who might have answers to my questions.

Mom sat in front of her computer at the kitchen table. There was a document open. She'd type a word, then delete it, so I could tell she was working on a poem. Maybe an elegy. Maybe a sestina. Hard to say. She had published a freestyle, non-rhyming bit in a magazine a few months ago, which she was really excited about. It was called "Alone." I'd asked her to read it to me, and she tried to, but every time she reached the third word, she'd burst into tears, so I hadn't gotten the full gist of it yet. My assumption: it was about Dad.

Writing poems was the only way Mom would discuss Dad—and by *discuss* I meant vaguely reference, but not talk about.

No one brought up Dad in conversation anymore. No one would reminisce or tell funny stories about him. As soon as the word *Dad* left your lips, Gracie and Mom started crying. And not just ladylike tears flowing down cheeks. I'm talking, like, gripping each other and needing three boxes of tissues and becoming pools of snot-grossness.

I didn't mind the tears... if it meant they would talk about Dad. But they wouldn't. They would shut down the conversation, saying, "Let's not talk about it. It's just too sad, Lana." Duck was less emotional, but she would frown and get uncharacteristically quiet. Her shoulders would slump, and they'd stay like that for the next few hours.

So it was an unspoken rule in our house now: Don't talk about Dad. Don't bring him up, even if it feels like he's slipping away. Don't make the others cry.

I had to handle this carefully. The envelope had his name on it, after all.

"Hi, Mom. Whatcha up to?" I asked in a light voice.

"Writing," she said. She didn't turn around or take her fingers off the keyboard.

"A poem?"

Her lips folded into a thin line and then the bottom one trembled. She didn't answer. She looked like she didn't dare say a word.

Which basically answered my question. It was a poem, and it was about Dad.

Two years and a month had taught me not to push her. Not if I wanted information. "Cool," I said. "I hope your writing goes well."

"Thanks, dear." It sounded like her throat was clogged with sand.

Oh boy.

"I actually wanted to talk about something else," I said. "I was wondering about the Alligator Witch."

Mom nodded, grabbed a tissue from the box on the table, blew her nose. "What about her?" After she wiped her nose and tucked the tissue away, her voice sounded normal again, so that was good. Also, she squinted at her computer screen and then deleted a word. Also good. We were making progress, even if her poem wasn't.

"Do you think she's real?" I kept my voice sounding casual. No need to raise suspicion by bringing up the note. Not yet.

She said, "I don't know."

"But people believe in her, right? Isn't it, like, a thing to believe in her, around town?"

"You're not allowed in that marsh," she said, and she raised a hand from the keyboard to wag a warning finger at me.

"Got it. But why is everyone so scared of the marsh? If no one's sure if she's real or not, why worry?"

Mom looked thoughtful, tilting her head at her computer screen before turning to face me. "I honestly don't know, honey. Lots of people who live here believe in the witch, but you're right. No one has seen her, as far as I know."

"So she might be nice?"

"Who knows," Mom said. "There might not be anything out in that marsh besides a bunch of grass and bugs and alligators."

"You think it's all made up?"

"It *could* be," Mom said. "Well, not the part about alligators. They're definitely out there. So no going in that marsh."

"How can we find out if she's real or not?"

"We can't," Mom said, and she shrugged her shoulders, like that was that.

"But, Mom...," I said, and, yes, I whined because I wanted to know more, and I was sick of her shutting down conversations. "There has to be someone who knows, someone who's been out there."

Mom blinked at me and said, "You know, there is someone. I doubt that she's ever gone into the marsh, but she talks a lot about the witch, and, actually, one of us should pay her a visit."

"Oh?" Where was Mom going with this?

Mom got up, grabbed her phone, and started tapping at it. "Mrs. LaSalle," she said, and I could tell she had just pressed Send on a message. "Her rent is due." Her phone pinged. "Good news," she said, "she's home. You can pick up the check from her and ask her all you want about that witch."

"Uh," I said because I wanted information and, sure, I'd been to the LaSalles' house before, but this conversation was moving in an unexpected way, and it suddenly felt like I was being roped into a chore.

Mom rubbed her hands together, a sure sign that she had made up her mind.

Great.

"It will be perfect," she said. "Two birds with one stone. I get the rent. You get your questions answered."

She marched to the front door, held it open for me, and gestured like I should go out.

Okay, this was happening. Fine. Nothing to do but roll with it. "Got it," I said. At least I might get more information.

The door shut behind me, and I was off—down the long set of stairs, down the front walkway, and into the Texas sun.

The LaSalle house was on the other side of Nana's. It was hot, walking along the side of the road. There are no sidewalks on our street, and no houses except for these three—ours, Nana's, and the LaSalles'. Just three houses in a row and the marsh behind them and a few palm trees, which didn't offer nearly enough shade.

Our neighborhood, if you could call it that, was unusual for Galveston. Most of town had properties clustered close together, with little to speak of in terms of a yard, but we owned all the land that bordered the marsh and then some. We had since... well, as far as I knew, since forever. Someone—maybe my great-great-grandfather—had bought it all and built the three houses. My family still owned the marsh and the land and everything nearby.

The LaSalles' house was pink. Nana's was light green, and ours was baby blue. A beachy, island vibe even though what we had nearby couldn't be called a beach. For that, you needed to exit our neighborhood, hang a left, and drive a few miles down Seawall Boulevard.

I went up the LaSalles' porch stairs and knocked at the door. Waited. Then knocked again.

Mrs. LaSalle creaked open the door and, once she saw it was me, said, "Hello, Lana. Come in." She opened the door wider.

She was tall and had a round, open face with rapidly blinking eyes. She was older than Mom, and I thought she was retired, though what she had done for work, I had no idea.

I stepped inside and she shut the door behind me.

The LaSalle place was unsettling, but I couldn't tell you exactly why. The furniture was where it should be, and everything was neat and clean, with cross-stitched Bible verses on the walls. Still, I got goosebumps as soon as my feet hit the living room rug. Every time. Maybe it was the smell. Once you went inside, a musty smell pushed up your nose; a hint of sweetness laid somewhere underneath it that always made me think of death. Yup, complete goosebump material.

"Let me get you that check," Mrs. LaSalle said, and she went into the kitchen, maybe to grab her checkbook.

I gulped. It was now or never. "I was wondering," I called, and my voice came out high and tinny.

"Yes?"

"Do you know anything about the Alligator Witch?"

"Ah, yes," Mrs. LaSalle said, "your mother told me you might want to talk about her. Let me take you to the residential expert."

I didn't know what she meant, but when she said, "Come with me," and moved down the hall, I followed.

In the back bedroom there was a woman even older than Mrs. LaSalle. She sat in a rocking chair facing the window. Her hands rested on a cane in front of her. She had long hair that was white and braided so that a plait ran over her shoulder and fell onto her lap.

"You've met my mama before," Mrs. LaSalle said—although I didn't think I had. "You ask her whatever you want. She's the expert on the Alligator Witch."

That's when I noticed that news articles were thumbtacked to the wall, all about the witch. The headline nearest me read, "Witch Fires Freeze Three." The next one read, "Alligator Witch Festival Doomed from the Start." Another one: "Experts Agree: Tornado Linked to the Witch." There were drawings too, and Polaroid pictures, and what looked like old documents—all attached to the walls with colorful thumbtacks.

"Whoa," I breathed.

If Dad was here, he'd have a conniption. *Those documents should be in a museum*, he would have said. *Or at least stored behind glass.* He would also have complained about the small holes created by the thumbtacks.

On the other hand, he'd be in love with the history, and he'd probably want to stop in front of each scrap of paper and give it a good look-over.

Mrs. LaSalle—the younger one—stepped in, toward the older one—Grandma LaSalle—and spoke in an extra loud voice: "Mama, Lana Parker is here. You remember her. Amelie's girl. One of the twins. She's gonna ask you about the Alligator Witch."

When you're a twin, fraternal or not, people group you together. So I was never just Lana Parker. I was Lana Parker, the twin, or Gracie's twin sister, or, as she said, one of the twins.

Grandma LaSalle nodded like she understood, and Mrs. LaSalle scooted around me, returning the way she'd come. I took another step into the room. The smell in here was stronger than in the living room, and new goosebumps broke out on my arms.

This old lady was clearly fascinated with the Alligator Witch, but a close second—in terms of obsessions—was religion. If a Holy War was coming, this was where the first battle would rage. There were crosses everywhere. Golden ones. Silver ones. Ones with flowers on them for decoration, and ones with wreaths of vines and thorns. Sitting next to her on a table was a silver cross that looked dangerous. Its long end had been sharpened to a point, like you could stab someone with it.

Holy crumbs.

Grandma LaSalle turned my way and said in a creaky voice, "Come closer."

The story of Hansel and Gretel popped into my mind, and I started shaking, but I pushed my fear away. This woman was old, sure, ancient, and maybe paranoid, but she wasn't going to stab me. I doubted she could stand up quick enough to take me by surprise. Besides, she had information about the witch, and I needed her help, so I had to be brave.

"Hello, ma'am," I said in a loud voice.

"You want to know about the Alligator Witch?"

"I do."

"You know not to go in that marsh, to never go in there?" Her voice sounded dusty, like she hadn't used it in twenty-five years.

I said, "Yes, ma'am. I know."

"She's a powerful being, that witch."

"Yes, ma'am."

"Not human any longer." Grandma LaSalle turned back to the

window and gazed out with narrowed eyes as if she was a guard on duty. Her view looked right into the marsh.

"That's her house, right?" I said, and I pointed to the one stand of trees that was visible.

She nodded but didn't speak, so I thought I should go for it. Just start asking the questions I came to ask. Here was the first: "You say she was powerful and not quite human and that I shouldn't go in the marsh, but what if someone was supposed to do something with her? I think my dad was supposed to go see her before he died." I let out a breath. It was kind of nice to talk about my dad with someone. I wasn't worried about this woman bursting into tears or asking me to stop mentioning him.

"Your father would never go see that witch." She said this like she was certain.

"But what if he had to for some reason?" I challenged. "What if he had an important thing to do? Like a duty?"

She turned to stare at me, and her eyes were whiter than they should have been. It was so startling, I held my breath. Was she blind? Or was she a witch too? Maybe coming here was a mistake.

"Your father knew what that witch is capable of," she said.

"And what is that?" I asked. "What can she do?"

Grandma LaSalle let her gaze swing back toward the window, and I found I was relieved. It felt like she'd looked inside me, with those too-white eyes, seen every thought I'd ever had, good or bad.

"She was a medium. She terrorized all of Galveston, wreaking havoc on the city with her evil ways." She tapped her cane against the rug. "I'm betting you don't know what a medium is." She didn't wait for me to answer. (Hint: I didn't know.) "A medium is someone who can look past the veil and see into the spirit world. Someone who can talk to the dead."

My breath caught in my throat.

"A medium would hold a ceremony called a séance," Grandma LaSalle continued, her voice getting stronger. "During the séance she would contact the dead and tell everyone what those who'd passed were saying."

"Can the Alligator Witch speak with the dead—now? Still?"

She answered, "If she's alive, maybe." Grandma LaSalle smiled a kind of creepy smile. "But she's not alive."

"She's dead?"

"*She's in between*," she said with emphasis. "That's why she's even more powerful than before, see? She's not in the land of the living, but she hasn't passed over yet. She has access to both worlds."

Spit gathered in my mouth, and I gulped. It was weird to think about—someone not alive or dead.

She said, "From the in-between, she prowls the island, looking for live things."

I recognized this as part of a song.

When the weather turns bad,
And when the rain clings,
The Witch comes around
Prowling for live things—

"So don't be no live thing near her," Grandma LaSalle said. "Good weather or bad."

That last part made me take a small step back. "Yes, ma'am."

Mrs. LaSalle—the younger one—showed up then with a soft

knock on the open bedroom door. "You got your questions answered, Lana?"

I nodded. I wanted to say something—*yes, ma'am*, maybe—but my voice stayed stuck in my throat.

"Okay, then. Here's your check. You run on back and give it to your mama."

I was more than happy to oblige. I made it home in record time, out of breath and sweating like it was going out of style.

Chapter Six

That night, I lay in bed and held the key above my head, dangling it down by the blue ribbon. It twirled in small, lazy circles. Tofu jumped onto the bed near my head and watched it with me. He lifted a paw as if he'd swat it. But he didn't. He watched it go around and around with his paw up and ready.

"What do you open?" I asked the key. "What was Dad going to do with you?" I turned to look at Tofu. "What do you think, buddy?" He didn't answer—of course he didn't—but sat like a cat statue, before growing bored and jumping down.

I laid the key on my pillow and shifted onto my side so I could see it. A key in profile. Just a sliver of gold. In my mind, my dad could open all kinds of things with it—locks, treasure chests, ancient trunks, suitcases that were so old and banged up they might have been through World War II. Each time he turned the key and opened a container, his face grew happy. It was the closest I'd felt to him for a long time.

"The witch would know what you open," I said to the key.

Then, I remembered something that Grandma LaSalle had said: The Alligator Witch could talk to the dead. She had access to both worlds.

That meant the witch could talk to Dad.

She wasn't dead—not quite—but Dad was. He was gone. I could never ask him anything. But the witch...

After I fell asleep, I dreamed and dreamed and dreamed of her.

Chapter Seven

I have written this account of Zofia Kowalczyk to the best of my ability, trying to stay as close to the truth as possible. Alas, for the rest, I was forced to use my imagination! Only Zofia knows it all.

If we have learned anything from Mr. Henry James, it is that a narrator sitting, as it were, on the left shoulder of a protagonist brings out much feeling. I hope that my narrative will inspire empathy in the reader—but more than that, I hope this narrative will clear Zofia's name one day.

I pray the truth will come out!

Zofia entered a pawn shop, her bag in hand. She had arrived on this island only a few days before, so she didn't know the shops well. But everyone she'd asked had told her this one was the finest, most trusted in Galveston; if she had anything to sell, this was the place to go.

They were right. The shop was gorgeous. Not like the old, dusty places in New York City where the goods were grimy and stacked haphazardly. Here, the glass cases were so clean they nearly sparkled. The items for sale were orderly and laid on dark blue cloths to bring out their best features. Everything looked so new, and there were so many, many things to buy.

Without meaning to, Zofia stepped toward a case holding rings and necklaces. She didn't wear much jewelry herself—she had never had the money to wear it—but it was beautiful to look at. Below her fingers were the most gorgeous things she'd ever seen. Fine ladies must have worn them once. Fine ladies, indeed, must have sold them to the pawnbroker.

A faint cough made her glance up. A young lady about her age was in the shop too. Zofia had missed her standing there before. She had on a light yellow dress with frills and pearls around the neckline. Her hair was done in intricate curls and held up by . . . Zofia didn't even know. She would think it was magic if she didn't know better. Maybe some kind of clips? The young woman smiled at Zofia and walked toward her.

Zofia felt self-conscious. What if she said something wrong or did something wrong? The thought made her fidget with the handle of her bag.

The young lady stopped and bent over the same counter, so she was close to Zofia. "Pretty, aren't they?" she asked. "I'm considering getting that broach." She pointed at an item in the case. "Mr. Abrams is asking a dollar for it. A full dollar. What do you think?" She glanced up at Zofia. "I believe that might be real ivory, but it's difficult to tell. I asked him to check the paperwork so I could be sure."

Zofia stood still for a moment. She wasn't sure how to answer! She tried to remind herself that this was just another young woman, like her. Zofia shouldn't be scared—new to town or not. She turned to consider the broach. A burnt rose background. A woman's profile in white in the foreground. The white part was shiny, but she didn't think it was ivory.

As she looked, a nearby spirit presented itself to her—wispy and ethereal. It was a kind spirit, so Zofia listened to what it said.

"You might do better with that ring," Zofia said, and she pointed to the band with a beautiful red gem. "It looks like a genuine garnet."

"You have a good eye," the young lady said.

A man came through a door, one that led to a back room. He was all smiles.

"Miss Getty," he said, addressing the woman beside Zofia, "good news."

The spirit in the room let out a loud grunt. Well, loud to Zofia. Though she could hear the dead, she knew most others couldn't.

To her, the spirit's message was clear: this man was not to be trusted.

"I have to tell you, I'd forgotten which customer sold this to me." The man bonked his head with his hand like he was the silliest creature on earth. "But looking at the paperwork brought it all back. That broach—not only is it all ivory, but it had been in the family for generations."

The spirit grumbled something about lies.

"She didn't want to sell it to me," he said with an exaggerated shrug. "But I gave her such a good price, she relented."

The spirit barked out a loud, "Ha!" and turned to face the man. "Mr. Abrams, you offered her three pennies and if she hadn't been so down on her luck—"

Zofia watched the spirit, wondering what it would do, but it didn't seem like it was going to make any mischief. It probably lived here. Maybe it had sold a piece of jewelry to him and liked to stay close to it in death.

"I'm glad to sell the broach to you. A dollar is a bargain price," Mr. Abrams said to the young woman, the one he'd called Miss Getty.

"I think I'd rather have that ring," Miss Getty said. She pointed to the one with the garnet. The one Zofia had suggested.

"Oh," the owner said, and his face fell briefly before lighting up again. "That one. Yes, a good selection, a fine selection, but it will cost you two dollars, I'm afraid."

Miss Getty cocked her head to the side. "You told me before that the broach was the most expensive item in this case."

"Oh, well," Mr. Abrams huffed.

Zofia stood up straight. "I'm new to Texas, but I hope this isn't one of those establishments like you'd find in New York City. The shop owners there were notoriously immoral. They'd swindle a grandmother out of her last dime." She turned to Miss Getty. "This isn't one of those types of places, is it?"

"I certainly hope not," Miss Getty said. Her words were aimed at Mr. Abrams.

Both women turned to look at the shop owner, who coughed into his hand. "This is an honest shop," he said. "I give you my word."

In the end, Miss Getty was able to talk Mr. Abrams into letting her have the ring for half the cost of the broach—fifty cents. The spirit in the room cheered, announcing to all who could hear (that was, Zofia) that it was a bargain.

Zofia followed Miss Getty out of the shop. She wasn't going to sell anything to the likes of Mr. Abrams. She had a feeling that he wouldn't offer her a good price. And she still had a few coins in her purse. Enough to last another day or two.

"I hope you enjoy your new purchase," Zofia said to Miss Getty out on the sidewalk. Miss Getty had already placed the ring on her finger, and she was turning it in the sunlight, perhaps admiring its shine. "It looks brilliant on you," Zofia added.

Miss Getty smiled at Zofia. "It certainly is a good fit. Now I just need a red dress to go with it."

She must be rich, Zofia surmised, to be thinking about a new dress right after spending a whole fifty cents on a ring.

The young woman held out her hand. "I'm Abigail. Abigail Getty."

"A pleasure to meet you." They shook. "I'm Zofia."

"Lovely." Abigail's face was bright. She looked up and down the street as if she'd lost something. "Now there's just the problem of my sister."

"Problem?"

"I'm afraid so." She rolled her eyes. "There's always a problem with my sister." She said this good-naturedly, as if her sister really was a problem but she was trying to make the best of it. "She ran off while I was shopping." Her head swiveled back and forth. "Now where could Libby have gone?"

"Do you want me to help you look?" Zofia asked.

"No, no. She's bound to turn up." Abigail spoke in a happy tone, but it sounded forced. "Ah, there she is," she said after a cart moved off and one could see down the street clearly. A smartly dressed young lady had exited a building labeled Guidestone Charity. "Light of my life," Abigail said.

This was sarcasm—Zofia was sure of it.

Abigail's sister, Libby, stomped up the street. She looked vastly different from Abigail. Whereas Abigail was slender and fragile-looking, Libby was sturdy and wide. Abigail seemed to float. Libby moved with purpose.

"Do you have other siblings?" Zofia asked.

"A brother. He's a year younger."

"Do you get along well with them?"

"If one must have a sibling, then a brother will do. I wouldn't advise a twin sister, though," Abigail said.

Zofia cocked her head to the side, taking in the information. "You and Libby are—" It seemed unthinkable; they were so different.

"Twins, yes," Abigail said with a sigh. "Fraternal." She produced a handkerchief and fanned herself with it. "Join me for lunch this week?"

Zofia's heart nearly stopped. She wanted to go—she desperately wanted a friend—but it might be expensive, and she didn't have much money.

Her emotions must have zipped across her face because Abigail hastily added, "My treat, of course. I would love to hear about New York City. That's where you're from, correct?"

"Yes."

"I need to hear everything, absolutely everything about it. You'll join me, won't you?" She looked enthusiastic and perhaps as eager for companionship as Zofia was.

"I would be glad to," Zofia said. "Thank you for the invitation."

Libby approached them and sounded annoyed with her sister when she said, "New friend?"

"Yes," Abigail said. "This is Zofia. I'll be taking her to lunch later this week. You're welcome to join us if you'd like."

Libby's eyes moved over Zofia—from feet to head. She made a scoffing sound.

Abigail dabbed at her brow with her handkerchief. "You don't need to be rude, Lib. A simple 'no thank you' would suffice."

"I wasn't being rude," Libby countered. "I just don't think Father would...approve."

Zofia's stomach clenched. Why wouldn't someone approve of her? Certainly her dress was old and not right for a Texas island in the summer, but could he really—?

Abigail's words, said cooly, cut off the thought: "Father wouldn't approve of me making a new acquaintance and introducing her to the sights of the town? Or he wouldn't approve of me welcoming a newcomer to our lovely island? Zofia's from New York City."

Libby plastered an obnoxiously pretend smile on her face and nodded at Zofia. "My apologies. I didn't mean to sound impolite."

"No apology necessary," Zofia said in a quiet voice.

"Well, with that settled," Abigail said, tucking that handkerchief away and pressing her hand against Zofia's, "we'll see each other soon. Where are you lodging? I'll come call on you."

Zofia was embarrassed of her cheap boardinghouse, but she gave Abigail the establishment's name.

"Good. I'll come by Tuesday? Say noon?"

That was fine with Zofia, and she said as much. She had no other plans before then, except to try to make some money. Perhaps she could put on a street performance or offer a séance.

Zofia watched the twins saunter away after that. Never would she have believed that they were twins if she hadn't heard Abigail say so herself. They were so different—in manner, in conversation, in physicality, and even in gait.

Quite surprising indeed, she thought to herself as she turned to make her way back to the boardinghouse and her room.

Even more surprising was the happiness she felt.

She might have made her first friend in Galveston.

Chapter Eight

When I woke, I couldn't quite remember my dream, and I felt tingly all over. It had been something about the Alligator Witch flying through the air, while I stood in the marsh, watching her in wonder.

Dreaming. Sleep. Last night.

The key!

I patted my pillow and then patted it again. Where was it? I had fallen asleep with the key next to my head. I sat up, hopped off my bed. Scampered around until I spotted it. There. Under the bedframe. It must have slipped off during the night.

"I'm glad I found you," I whispered to that golden key as I wrapped my hand around it. "I'll keep you safe." I pulled the ribbon around my neck. It was soft against my skin, and the perfect length—like it was meant to be there.

I got dressed and tucked the envelope with Dad's note in my pocket. Gracie's music echoed through the wall. *Bump, bump, bump.* A strong drumbeat. A high-pitched voice. K-pop.

Again.

Mom and Duck were in the living room, sitting in nearly the same positions I had found them in yesterday. The only change was Duck's pj's. She had on a fresh set: little penguins, rather than a Minecraft design.

I shook my head. This was too much.

It wasn't just déjà vu. It was a repeat. A total and complete repeat. Like I was in one of those movies where the main character has to live through the same day again and again and again.

I considered asking Mom if we could go somewhere, but I already knew what the answer would be. Same as yesterday. Too hot, too many tourists.

I didn't waste my breath.

Instead, I pulled on my sneakers and tapped Mom on the shoulder. "I'm going outside."

She removed an earbud. "What?"

I repeated, "I'm going outside."

"To Nana's?"

"Just outside."

I was already thinking about the marsh. My dream had inspired me. I wanted to see that witch.

Despite the warnings.

Despite what Grandma LaSalle had said.

Despite what Nana and everyone else had always said.

Because that witch was the only one who could help. The only one who could possibly talk to Dad. Ask him what he was supposed to do before he died. Ask him about his duty. Ask him about this key.

Mom nodded, and I kept a blank look on my face as I moved to the door. Tofu was sprawled in front of it, because of course he was.

"Hey, buddy," I said to him, "would you mind moving your big ole kitty butt?"

He lifted his head, blinked at me, then laid it back down.

I cracked open the door, so he'd know I was serious. "Buddy," I said. Nothing. No movement. "Tofu. I'm going to open this. It's going to knock into you."

He stayed put.

If I was going to walk into that marsh, I wanted to get going. Sure, it was still morning, but I had slept in. Everyone was already up. I checked my phone. Nearly ten o'clock. If I was going to go, I should leave pronto. Before everything became as hot as the inside of a hair dryer.

But should I?

The question lingered.

I bit my bottom lip. First things first, I'd go outside and check out the electric fence. See if I could get past it. Next, I'd consider the rest.

If Tofu would get out of the way.

"Tofu, really," I said, and I pulled the door so that it pushed against his soft kitty back end. He must have figured out that I meant business, because he got up and stretched. Still in the way. "Buddy..." Was I losing patience? Sure, but only as much as you could with a cute cat—which is to say, no, not really. Plus, I'd lived with Tofu a long time and I knew his scoop. He'd get the gist and scoot out of the way eventually.

When I swung the door again and gave his backside a *tap-tap*, he finally trotted off.

"Thanks, bud," I called over my shoulder.

The fence was in the backyard, where the grass ended, and the brown muck began. You knew where it was because electricity filled the air. The hair on your arms stood up, and if you got close enough, you'd get a shock.

I'd always given that fence a good ten-foot perimeter out of respect for its ability to possibly flatten me.

But today was a different story.

The fence was a good two feet tall; if I stood next to it, it would come up just past my knees, so I'd have to jump high and be brave.

I leaped into the air a few times, seeing how high I could go. Soccer season had finished up in May but all spring, Coach had had us work on our jumps. "Heading the ball takes height," she said. "You've got to propel your body high into the air." The jump that I needed today was a little different. Less straight up and down, more spanning some distance, but at least I'd had *some* practice. On the other hand, it had been a few months and between you and me, I thought I'd probably get zapped here to kingdom come.

Was it worth it?

I took the key out from where it hung under my shirt. If the witch was real, she'd have answers. She could talk to Dad, so I decided that yes, it was.

It was me versus the fence. Me versus electricity and/or me versus the pull of gravity.

I inched toward the wire and held my breath. I figured when the hair on my arms stood up, I'd know where to jump from.

But nothing happened. Every little hair stayed down and the ground beneath my feet didn't buzz.

I took another step. The wire was only a few inches in front of me. I should feel it. I should get that don't-come-any-closer thing.

But I didn't.

Maybe the fence was off.

I scanned its length. It looked intact.

I pushed my foot even closer. I was so near I could touch it.

What would happen if I did? Burns? Pain? Just a small shock? I wasn't sure.

Gulping in a breath for courage, I reached out. The wire was warm to the touch, but only from the sun.

Fabulous. This was a clear sign I should go see that witch. I held down the wire and stepped over it, glad I didn't have to test my high jump today.

Next possible problem: alligators.

I took a minute to consider what I knew:

- Alligators were deadly, but mostly when they got you under water, and here, in the marsh, there wasn't much water. Not deep water, anyway. I should be fine unless one dragged me all the way to West Bay.
- Alligators could bite. Their jaws were strong. How strong? I didn't know, but it seemed like bad news to have to find out.
- Alligators had short, stumpy legs. Their skin was like armor. They had tons of teeth. They had been around since the time of dinosaurs.

Here's what I didn't know:

- How fast an alligator could run.
- What I should do if I bumped into one. For instance, should I dash away as fast as possible, or run all zigzag, or stay still and call for help?

Hmm, not good. Some important stuff on the "didn't know" list.

Conclusion: I'd try my best not to bump into an alligator.

I headed into the muck, making a beeline for that stand of trees.

All around me, the marsh was alive. There were hidden, living things everywhere. Cicadas buzzed from the grass. Beetles clicked and birds chirped, though I couldn't see them. One would sound and then stop when I got close. Another would start up and, again, stop when I approached. Dragonflies flitted from grass top to grass top, and pond skimmers danced on the edges of puddles.

And the bugs. There were, to sum it up, a lot of them. Mostly mosquitoes.

They buzzed around my ears. One landed on my shin. As I batted it away, a line of blood smeared on my leg. Another one stuck my forearm, and another landed on my hand even though I swatted at it. They were everywhere—on my face, neck, legs, even on the top of my head. Ugh. I should have used bug spray. Like, coated myself in it. Taken a bath in it, maybe. I was going to be itchy tomorrow, that was for sure.

As I walked, the sun beat down, growing hotter and angrier by the second, and in no time, mud ringed my sneakers. Sweat gathered *everywhere*. I could feel it underneath my shirt and on the back of my neck and on my face.

Gross.

Something growled to my left and that low, rumbly sound made me stop, statue-still. If you've ever heard an alligator make a noise like that, then you know what I'm talking about and why I put on the brakes.

Where was it?

A swishing noise sounded, and a clump of reeds nearby waved like something had pushed through them.

I waited but heard nothing else. Despite the heat, I shivered, and I had to give myself an intense internal pep talk to start off again.

When I got close to the stand of trees, I paused. The marsh had gone quiet. Suddenly, there were no noisy bugs, no annoying mosquitoes, no birds, no dragonflies. It was like that part of the marsh was in a different country—one that was deserted or dead.

I couldn't see a witch anywhere. Or a house. Just a stand of trees, their branches twisty and thin, prickly and thorny. Had this been a colossal waste of time? Maybe.

"Hello?" I called.

A sound I didn't expect to hear filled the air.

Scratch! Screech! Scrape!

The trees were moving. Not from the wind—there was no wind. Yet they jumbled themselves together, intertwined and straightened and re-formed. My pulse sped up like my blood wanted to escape my veins. Sweat dripped down the back of my neck. Those branches moved and tangled and straightened some more and then there was a house. It had formed out of the trees. Siding and a window and a front door.

It stood on alligator legs.

Chapter Nine

Lots of houses around here were on stilts because people worried about floods. The Big Storm of 1900 killed nearly 8,000 people. But I'd never seen a house up on alligator legs.

The witch was real, and I'd found her. Wow—oh wow!

"Hi there," I called. "Is anyone home?" I'd forgotten my fear and felt only an anxious anticipation. I'd have answers soon. "I'd like to talk to the Alligator Witch, please," I said, and I held my chin high. I tugged that key from around my neck and gripped it tight.

The knob on the front door turned and *creak!* the door swung open. Steps unfolded themselves down to the ground.

Whoa.

A young woman appeared in the doorway and descended to the first step. She studied me, so I gave her the once-over too. Her dress was long and old-fashioned looking, and her brown hair was pulled up in a bun. The dress was deep red and black, with trim and ruffles. You couldn't pay me to wear that—because it was fancy but also because it was waaay too hot outside. She looked like a nice person, or almost nice.

"Speak your business, girl of the town." Her voice had an edge to it. She didn't trust me.

"I, uh, uh...," I stammered, not sure how to answer. "I'd like to learn what this key is for." I held it out so she could see. "It belonged to my dad, and he had some kind of duty he was supposed to complete before he died but I can't ask him what it was because...well, he's dead. I was hoping you could contact him for me and find out."

Again, I felt the relief that came with talking about my dad without the fear of someone bursting into tears or telling me to stop. But something changed in her face, then. She didn't look nice anymore.

"You want me to talk to the dead?" she asked. That edge in her voice grew razor sharp.

"Uh..." She seemed to be waiting for an answer. "If you don't mind?"

An unworldly wind whipped up. It was cold, and it blew against me, the alligator house, the lady dressed in old-fashioned clothes. The color of her dress faded. The fabric frayed and became ragged. Her hair changed too, turning white and frizzy.

"Shall I contact the spirits, girl of the town?" She yelled this, maybe to be heard over the wind. Maybe because she was angry.

In that moment, I saw her as Mrs. LaSalle had described—she was the witch and she was a being not dead but not alive. She was somewhere in between, and she might start prowling for live things, just like the song said.

I was alive.

Holy crumbs. This was a mistake. I had made a huge mistake.

My heart jumped and bumped and squeezed in my chest in such a way I thought it might be trying to break all my ribs.

"I'll give you all this town deserves," the witch said, and her eyes turned black. No whites. No color. Two black voids. She flew up and over the steps and landed on the ground near me. She could fly!

I held my body still, too scared to move, clinging to Dad's key.

She leaned close to me, and I'll tell you something, that witch was *cold*. Being near her felt like I was standing in front of an AC blower, which maybe, because of the heat, should have been nice but it wasn't. "I'll give you all this town deserves," she repeated, this time whispering it near my ear. Her icy breath rained on my cheek.

My knees wanted to buckle, but if I fell to the ground, she would pounce on me. She might kill me. So I kept myself upright—somehow.

She backed up a step and shouted, "Spirits, show yourselves."

Noises pounded through her house. It sounded like a band was playing, but the house wasn't big enough. Plus, it would have been the worst band ever. Less music than chaos. A tambourine shook and clapped. An accordion creaked and groaned. Someone or something slammed their fists on every wall.

The band took its act outside. The tambourine appeared at the open door. No one was holding it, but somehow it hovered four feet in the air. It was flying, just like the witch. I sucked in a scream when the instrument hurled down the stairs and came to a stop in front of me. An accordion was next. Silver and red with black handles. Played by ghost hands. A candelabra followed, flying down. It had three prongs and three candles and three flames dancing above the wicks.

The witch said, "These are my spirits, girl of the town. They do my bidding."

I didn't dare say a word. Only my knees shook, and my breath came out in little whistling puffs.

She raised her voice. "Flames, come." The flames flew off the candlesticks and floated in the air. The witch waved her hands near them, over them, through them. "These cannot be destroyed, you see. They're magic." She blew out a big breath, like she was trying to put out birthday candles, but they stayed lit. "Flames, yes, but they have freezing power. Whomever they choose to infect will be caught in their spell."

Infect? I didn't like that word. It sounded like a virus, and I wasn't a fan of viruses. I knew what kind of damage they could do.

"These three flames will take three souls," the witch said. "The three souls that you love."

She got taller, then, growing many feet; her body stretched out weirdly. She glared down at me.

I shouldn't have come here. Grandma LaSalle had warned me. Mom had warned me. Nana had always told me not to. I'd heard the song growing up. But I hadn't listened. Not to any of them.

Stupid. Impulsive.

Ugh.

The witch was not going to help, and Dad felt further away than ever.

"The souls will belong to me," she said, and her voice was deeper, rougher than before. "I'll freeze them in time. I'll freeze them and they'll be mine."

The air zapped out of my lungs and stayed gone. I couldn't inhale, exhale. I couldn't do anything. My eyes teared up, burning, as I realized what she'd said. She would take the souls of three people I loved. She would freeze them, and they would belong to her.

"No," I whimpered. Images of all those I loved whizzed through my head—Mom, Duck, Tofu, Nana, Gracie. Dad. "Please don't hurt them." My voice cracked.

There was a flicker of something in the witch. Like she had a good part and a bad part, and the good side had heard me. Or like she had a dead part and a living part, and the living one took a breath. She looked more solid. But then whatever happened undid itself, and she became all evil and death and unstable again like a bunch of dust held together by pure malice. She smiled, and it was a wolfish smile. "There is one thing," she said, and she rose higher, her body lengthening even more, "one thing that you could do to save them."

"Anything," I squeaked out.

"I will trade. Your souls for what's mine."

"What's yours?" I said, or tried to say. My voice was a hoarse whisper. "I don't understand."

With lightning speed, she was in my face. Breathing her cold breath on my cheeks and eyes and nose and chin and hanging over me like a vulture. "Give me back what's mine!" she shrieked.

"Where is it? Who has it?"

"Find Matthew, and you'll find what I need."

And then *Boom!* the witch and the instruments and the candlesticks were gone. The stairs to her house folded themselves back up and the door slammed shut. *Scratch! Screech! Scrape!* The house folded and tangled and creaked back into a stand of trees.

The three flames sped off, soaring through the air. They flew past me, and I was shaking so hard I fell into the mud. I got myself flipped over to watch the flames.

They were sailing over the marsh, headed toward my house.

Chapter Ten

Never had I so badly wished for Dad to be here again. He would have known what to do. He always did. "Help me," I whispered, hoping somehow that Dad's spirit was around.

But no one answered. The house was gone. The witch was gone. Only the stand of trees remained.

Panic gripped me. What had she said? Three souls would be hers. Three souls would be taken, frozen.

I stood. The flames, where were they? I put my hand up to block the sun and found them speeding over the marsh, rushing toward the three pastel-colored houses in the distance. My vision blurred from tears...

If Dad was here, he'd know what to do. He always did. He was the first one up on Thanksgiving morning, heading out the door at 7 a.m. for the local Turkey Trot. He was the first one to jump in a pool, even if someone warned him it was cold. He was the first in line to board a roller coaster—especially if it had a loop the loop. He was brave and decisive and amazing.

Me, all I could do was stand there in the mud, shaking, when I needed to be running.

Get going!

Run, feet, run!

When I finally got my body to obey, I threw the key around my neck and rushed after those flames. I dashed through the marsh, mud splattering the backs of my legs. I had to grab the tall grass to keep from slipping once, and the bugs were relentless. I paused only when I got to the wire.

Still no electricity. No shock. Not even a small deterrent.

I panted as I ran around to the front yard and bounded up the stairs, taking them two at a time. At the front door, I held the knob and let out a small, wet sob. I was scared of what I'd find inside.

I turned the handle and pressed on the door, which opened about eight inches. Something stopped it after that—a weight. No, a cat.

"Come on, Tofu." I didn't want to sound mean, but I needed that fuzzy guy to move. I had to get in. "Tofu, please." I pressed against the door harder. I gave him a *tap-tap*. Nothing. I pressed my weight against the door, and it slid... slowly. Little by little.

When I had enough clearance, I slipped inside and saw Tofu.

He was stretched out, lying on his side. His eyes were open, but he couldn't see me. He couldn't see anything. A flame danced over his fluffy kitty head.

I shut the door and crouched down next to him. New tears sprang to my eyes. I pet him on the stripes that covered his kitty forehead. His fur was cold. "Come on, sweet boy. Come on, buddy." I shook him gently. He didn't move or flinch or meow or even blink.

Was he dead? Had the witch killed him?

A second later I saw a sign of life. Breath. His body moved up and down as his lungs expanded and contracted. Thank goodness.

But alive or not, he was frozen. "I'm so sorry, Tofu. I hope it doesn't hurt." I gave him one more pat before standing. This was magic of the worst kind. Evil magic.

The warnings rang in my head again—*Don't go back there. The witch is dangerous.*

Grandma LaSalle—*That's why she's even more powerful than before, see?*

And Mom—*You're not allowed in that marsh.*

Even Nana—*Stay out of that marsh, Lana. She'll get you.*

I wished I had listened to them.

Something made a whirring sound in my ears. It grew louder, and my vision got dark around the edges. *Don't pass out*, I told myself. *That would only make things worse.*

I forced myself to breathe—in and out—and then I stepped farther into the house.

Deep down, though, I knew what I would find.

Mom and Duck were seated on the couch where I'd left them. Flames danced over their heads. Mom had a blank look on her face like she was still listening to that sappy audio book. Duck gripped her Switch. Her fingers didn't move. She was completely still.

Everything in me bubbled up, and I let out another sob. It was too much. Mom and Duck. My mom. My little sister. I had done this to them.

I had been so stupid.

"Mom?" I whimpered. I ran over to her and touched her face. She didn't move. She didn't even turn her eyes to meet my gaze. I let my fingers slide down her cold cheek. "I'm so sorry," I said.

I hurried over to Duck. Her game made familiar noises—a bunch of endermen or some kind of monsters were attacking her character. *Bash, bash!* I reached over and turned it off. Even though it didn't matter, I didn't want her to get killed while she was frozen. It didn't seem fair.

"I'm sorry, Duck." My bottom lip trembled, and a tear rolled down my cheek. I patted her shoulder like I wanted her to know I meant it. But just like Mom, she didn't respond. She couldn't. "I'll figure this out," I promised. "I'll help you."

I had to do something.

Gracie? Was she okay? Gracie!

I ran to my sister's room and flung open her door. She was on her bed, slouched low, her phone in her hand.

She glanced up at me. "Knock much?"

"Gracie," I sputtered, and spit actually went flying I was so happy to see her, so relieved she could move and talk and see me. "Gracie," I said again, but then I faltered. How do you tell a person that the rest of the family is frozen? "I, um…" My voice cracked.

She sat up straighter. "What? What's up with your clothes? OMG, is that mud? That is so gross."

"I…I…" I wanted the words to come out. I wanted to tell her what happened, but my throat felt like it was filled with cotton.

She looked worried, alarmed, even. "What?"

"I need your help," I said, or tried to say. It came out 50 percent squeak, 50 percent sheer desperation.

"Lana, what's going on?"

"Come with me." I beckoned her with a wave of my hand. Showing her would be easier than saying it out loud.

The hardest thing about being a fraternal twin was that everyone assumed you were best friends. This myth was reinforced by those movies starring those cute twin girls. They hung out together. They solved crimes together. They adored each other. Two peas in a pod. The best of friends.

Gracie and I were none of those things, and we never had been.

But it was hard to tell someone that. When they looked at you with a sparkle in their eyes and said, "So are you and your twin, like, best friends?" you couldn't say flatly, "No."

Twins were supposed to be best friends. Twins were supposed to be super close. Twins even had special twin superpowers. The ability to read each other's minds or feel each other's feelings.

Only, Gracie and I weren't close, and we certainly had no mental or emotional connection. We didn't even like the same things.

She liked love stories and social media and texting and K-pop. I liked math and playing soccer.

She was as close to being a vegetarian as you could get when you're twelve and you don't have control over the menu.

I would scarf down ten hamburgers in one sitting if Mom would let me.

We might have been closer if Gracie wasn't always so weepy. Ever since Dad died, that girl had been a fountain. Any little thing set her off crying. We'd never been close, but we'd grown even further apart in the last two years.

That's part of why I dragged my feet as I lumbered back toward the living room. Yes, I wanted Gracie's help, but I had a feeling I knew how this would go. Gracie would immediately start crying and I'd be on my own. She'd cry and cry and I'd have to figure it out by myself.

When we reached the living room, Gracie gasped. "What's—?" She stopped short. "What's going on?" She rushed to Mom, pausing about a foot from the couch and turning on her heel to stare at me. "Lana, what are those?" Gracie waved her hand at the flames.

"They're evil," I said. "Magic."

"Stop joking."

"I'm not."

"Mom," Gracie cried. "Mom!" She bent down close to Mom and shrieked, "Mom!"

I'd never heard Gracie yell so loud.

She waved her hand in front of Mom's face. She shook her by the shoulders.

I stopped Gracie by lightly touching her back. "Don't hurt her. She can't move."

"Can't move? Lana?" I could hear the fear in her voice. "What the heck? What's... what's wrong with her? What happened?" Her eyes filled with tears, as predicted. She seemed to notice Duck, then. "Her too?" Gracie ran over and grabbed Duck's game out of her hands. She looked like she was going to throw it down and then slap her to try to wake her up.

"Please don't," I yelped. "This is all my fault."

Gracie froze, but not like Mom and Duck. She was frozen with anger and pain and more emotions. Tears pooled in her eyes.

"I'm sorry," I said. I knew I had to talk quickly. If I didn't get a hold on Gracie at that second, she might go Total Tears on me. After Dad died, Gracie stayed in her room and cried for three days straight. She didn't eat, she didn't sleep, she didn't do anything but cry. If I'd had my license, I would have driven her to the hospital. It was that bad. Finally, she came out and drank some water, and Mom, thank goodness, emerged out of her own fog enough to get Gracie a sandwich.

Since then, it was touch and go with Gracie. Like when she found out Nana had the stroke. She disappeared into her room again and wept for hours. Thank goodness we were able to coax her out by dinnertime.

I couldn't let that happen again. I couldn't let Gracie go into some dark emotional hole, because I needed her help. Now. I didn't have time to spare.

It was me and her against this... this evil magic. The witch had taken Mom and Duck and Tofu. I had to keep Gracie from falling apart.

"It was my fault," I repeated. "I did something I shouldn't have. But we can fix this. Or, we can try, Gracie," I said. "We have to try."

Gracie's face was red. Her eyes were red. Her hair was messy. On a scale of one to ten, she looked like a negative two.

"Please help me," I begged.

Her face was a river of tears by this point, but I've got to hand it to her, she calmed her breathing with what looked like sheer willpower. "What did you do?"

Here it was. Time to come clean. I walked over to her, took Duck's Switch, and laid it on the coffee table before saying, "I went into the marsh."

Gracie gave a few shocked blinks. "You jumped over the fence?"

"The electricity was off, so I just climbed over."

"And you went into the marsh?" She sounded like she didn't believe me. Like she would never consider doing such a thing.

And she wouldn't. I was sure she wouldn't. If Gracie was anything, she was a rule-follower. She did what she was told.

"I found the witch," I said.

She shook her head like she was both astounded and confused by what she was hearing. "The Alligator Witch?"

"Yeah."

"She's real?"

I nodded.

"Like, real real?" Gracie asked.

I nodded again.

She blinked at me and wiped one cheek. "All this time I thought it was a story Nana made up."

"Well, she's real and she really doesn't like visitors from town."

Gracie's body trembled and shook. I waited for her to plop onto the floor and start sobbing, but again, she held it together. "So you bothered the Alligator Witch and she put those flames over Mom and Duck?"

"And Tofu." I gestured toward the door and her gaze followed.

Gracie made a noise in her throat. "Poor little guy," she said sadly.

"I know, right?" I huffed out a breath. "Gracie, I'm sorry. I'm really, really sorry."

She nodded and said, "How can we save them?"

I was so happy I almost hugged her. Because she was going to help. She was on board. Of course I didn't hug her because it was Gracie—and I wasn't the hugging type.

So, good. But now what? My mind went blank. I'd been riding high on adrenaline, and it took a minute of me going "uh" and "hold on" and "um" before my brain spun in the right direction and found what I needed. "The witch said she'd let the three souls go only if we returned what was hers."

"Three souls?" Gracie asked.

I counted on my fingers. "Mom, Duck, Tofu."

"What did you take that belongs to her?" she asked.

"Me? Nothing. But some guy named Matthew did."

Gracie took a step toward me. "Who's Matthew?"

"No idea."

"Well, then, what do we do? We can't ask Mom."

"I know," I said. "We're on our own."

Gracie nodded, looking grim. "Tell me again, exactly what she said."

"Sure, but..." I waved for her to follow me into my bedroom. It felt too weird to be talking about this in front of frozen Mom and Duck.

Gracie sat at my desk chair. I stood, since I was still covered in a bunch of muck from the marsh. "The witch said, 'Give me back what's mine.' If I do that, she said she'd free the three souls, and when I asked her where her stuff was, she said I should find Matthew."

"Give me back what's mine," Gracie muttered. "It doesn't make sense, and I don't know anyone named Matthew."

"Me neither," I said.

She paused, rubbing at her chin. "I can't think of any friends Mom might have named Matthew... but what about..."

"Dad?" I finished the thought for her. Dad taught history at the University of Houston. He had lots of colleagues. One of them could have been named Matthew, and because they all worshipped old stuff, maybe one of them had something belonging to the witch. Gracie's mouth crinkled and I sucked in a breath. *I shouldn't have mentioned Dad.* But she was headed in that direction, wasn't she?

Her throat moved in a way that looked painful, but she breathed in loudly through her nose, obviously trying not to cry. She said, "That's what I was thinking, actually. Matthew might be one of, you know, the people he used to work with."

"Yeah," I said, "I bet you're right."

She took in another big breath. "The question is," she said, holding her voice steady, "if Dad borrowed something from a guy named Matthew, where would it be?"

There was only one answer: his closet.

After Dad died, Mom gathered his things from around the house and shoved them in his closet. They were too hard to look at, she'd said. Better to have them out of sight with the door closed.

"Let's go see," Gracie said, and she straightened her back like she was ready for anything.

Holy cow, my sister was ready for anything.

Chapter Eleven

Gracie's phone pinged on our way through the house, because of course it did. If I could count on three things in the world, they were this:

- Duck loved Minecraft.
- Mom wrote poems and listened to sappy books and didn't take us anywhere during the summer.
- Gracie was on her phone 24/7. If she wasn't listening to music, she was texting someone. Most likely Nancy.

Gracie glanced down and read the message before beginning to type.

"Who is it?" I asked, suspicious.

"Nancy," Gracie said, and she said this like *Of course it's Nancy*.

Nancy was Gracie's best friend. They did everything together. They talked every day. They texted. They shared secrets. They were, in a word, inseparable. Summers were harder since Mom did her sit-on-the-couch thing, but they didn't let that get in the way of their friendship. Nancy had her mom schlep her over to our house, and her mom took them both out a bunch. Nancy's mom did whatever she asked.

Nancy... how do I put this? She wasn't my favorite person. She wasn't a bully or gossipy or anything like that. Basically the opposite. Nancy was super helpful. Eager. Enthusiastic. She was the first to offer assistance if a teacher needed anything. She was the first to volunteer for the school play or the class fundraiser or the extra credit spelling bee. If you needed a pencil, there was Nancy. Before you could even ask, she had a mechanical getup and specialty erasers from her bag held out for you. She was always like that. Like a puppy that wanted to be loved, but without the puppy cuteness. It rubbed me the wrong way. I guess I liked my friends like I liked my ice cream—chill.

"What's Nancy up to today?" I said, trying to keep the annoyance out of my voice because Gracie was holding it together and I was proud of her.

Gracie's face scrunched up in concentration as it often did when she was reading a text, doing something else (like walking, in this case), and trying to type at the same time. "Chores, and shopping at the Strand later. Her mom gave her a bunch of money for chocolate."

"That's nice," I said, but then it hit me. What was about to go down.

"Gracie," I said, and I blocked her way so she'd have to notice me. She needed to stop typing before it was too late. "You can't tell Nancy."

"What?" She glanced up as if surprised to find me there.

"You. Can't. Tell. Nancy. What's. Going. On," I said. I paused after each word, stretching the sentence out so Gracie would get it. This was important.

She looked baffled. "Why not? Nancy is super smart. She could help." Her fingers had stopped moving and that was good. That was a start.

"No," I said, "Nancy *cannot* help."

"But she might—"

I cut Gracie off. "Gracie, listen to me. She would call the police in a heartbeat."

Gracie still looked confused, and I pinched the bridge of my nose, searching inside myself to find the way to tell Gracie what she needed to hear. "Look, Nancy is..." I searched for the right word. "...a goody-goody. She does what she's told, and she does what she's supposed to do. Always. Just like you. I mean, besides maybe chowing down on way too much candy, she always does the right thing, you know?"

"That's not a bad quality...," Gracie said slowly. "She's a good person. What about it?"

"Listen." And I held up both hands. "What would you do in this scenario? Let's say the situation was reversed and Nancy called you and told you her mom and cat were frozen. What would you do?"

Nancy didn't have a dad as far as I knew, and she didn't have any siblings, so it wasn't quite the same. But she did have a cat. His name was Buster or Bruster or something like that.

Gracie turned to watch the ceiling for a moment, as if pondering.

"I'll tell you what you'd do," I said, snapping her focus back. "You'd call the cops. Or the fire department or some other official agency and try to get her help."

"Well, maybe," Gracie started.

I cut her off again because I was right and if she thought about it, she'd realize it. "Look, I know you would because you're also a good person, just like Nancy. You'd say to yourself, 'Nancy's mom and cat are frozen, so she needs help. She doesn't know what to do and I don't know what to do,' and in the next minute you'd be dialing 911." Gracie scratched the back of her neck like she was hesitating. I added, "Because you respect authority, and you'd want to help. Right?"

Still scratching her neck, she said, "Yeah, I guess so."

"So that's what Nancy would do too, right?"

"Okay." She sounded unsure.

"And if Nancy gets them involved, it's bad, Gracie. We're through. If she calls the cops, they'll come here and they'll see Mom and they'll find out that Nana is in a nursing home, and they'll do something. Like take us away and put us in foster care and then Mom and Duck and Tofu might stay frozen forever."

Gracie's hand flew to her mouth. This was sinking in.

"So you can't tell Nancy," I said, finishing strong. "If you do, she'll do something rash."

"What if I tell her it's a secret?" Gracie countered.

I tilted my head at her like *Come on*.

"She wouldn't tell anyone if I asked her not to," she argued. But you could tell by the look on her face and how Gracie now hugged her phone to her body that she knew the truth as well as I did. Nancy would tattle. Nancy was like that.

She slumped, giving up. "Fine. I won't say anything."

"Thank you," I said, and I started walking toward Dad's closet again.

I trusted her not to say anything. She'd given her word, and Gracie wouldn't break a promise.

Dad's closet door was shut, because of course it was. Mom didn't want to be reminded of him. Like Duck and Gracie, she wanted to forget about Dad, and it was hard to forget about a person with his stuff right there on your way to the bathroom. The door was always shut.

"Let's see what you might have from your friend Matthew, Dad," I said softly to myself.

I pulled the door open.

It was empty.

Completely empty.

There weren't any clothes or shoes or books or anything.

For about a month after he passed away, I would go into his closet and sit with his stuff, just trying to be close to him again. I'd put on his shirts and tie his sneakers onto my feet. I'd breathe in his smell, and even talk to him, like he could hear me. Like he was still there.

I hadn't done that in almost two years.

And now it was all gone.

"What the—?"

"What the—?" Gracie spouted from behind me.

So this was a surprise to her too.

I felt that hole in my insides open up again.

Mom had given his stuff away. Or gotten rid of it. Or redistributed it. I didn't know when, but I knew one thing: she hadn't asked us if we wanted anything.

She must have given some of it to Nana, though. That would explain his wallet and shirt and favorite books in her bureau.

"That is so not okay," Gracie said, and a tear ran down her face.

She was right. This was so *not* okay, but Mom and Duck and Tofu were frozen, and we had to stay focused. I had to keep us on track, despite my anger. Despite Mom's betrayal.

"If Dad did have something of the witch's," I said, "if one of his friends gave him something to hold, it's not here now." My voice cracked at that last part, so I cleared my throat and pumped my fist against my chest like I had indigestion and then started again. "No big deal. We just need a new plan." I slammed the closet door shut.

Gracie stood at in the bedroom doorway, looking at that closed door.

"Gracie," I said, "come on."

She nodded, turned, and trudged my way. "What are we going to do?" she asked, and she sounded broken.

My mind spun. "We're going to... we're going to..." I looked at Mom's bed and longed to throw myself on it or at least sit on it. But my clothes. "We're going to start by getting me into something clean," I said. "I really don't want to smell like a marsh's best friend anymore. And after that, we're going to figure out how to handle this."

"We need an Alligator Witch expert," Gracie said softly, with more than a hint of despair in her voice.

"Holy crumbs," I said, and I patted her on the shoulder because she was exactly right, and I wanted to bolster her spirits the way she had just bolstered mine. "You're a genius. I'm going to get changed and then we're going to go talk to an Alligator Witch expert."

Chapter Twelve

It was 11:30 when I pulled Gracie to a stop. We had to figure something out before heading up the LaSalles' front stairs. "We need a story," I said.

She gave me a look like she had no idea what I was talking about.

"Like, is this a school project or an extra credit assignment? Just like with Nancy, we can't tell the LaSalles the truth."

Understanding dawned on her face and then she looked scared. Scared like she might never have lied before. Like she didn't know how to do it. Ugh. She was such a rule-follower.

"Not a school project," Gracie mustered. "School's out and I bet even they know that."

"Good point."

"So, yeah, extra credit." She sounded unsure, still nervous. "Special summer extra credit."

"Excellent," I said, and I knew I'd have to be the one to say the words. Gracie wouldn't lie—not unless she absolutely had to.

Mrs. LaSalle took forever and a day to answer the door, like yesterday, but finally, there she was. "Oh, hello, girls."

"Hi, Mrs. LaSalle. Could I possibly talk to your mom again about the Alligator Witch?" I asked.

"Of course," she said.

"Gracie wanted to come too," I said as she let us in the house. "I didn't mention it before, but we have an extra credit project for school. It's one of those things that we have to do over the summer and when I told my sister how informative your mom was, she wanted to tag along."

Gracie shot me a look like that would never happen. She was right—she would have handled any summer assignment back in June. That was just how she was.

"I'm sure my mother would love to talk to you both." Mrs. LaSalle halfway turned to look at us and chuckled as she brought us down the hallway. "Sounds like they're giving more interesting summer projects than they did in my day."

"Yes, ma'am," I said.

Gracie cleared her throat like she was uncomfortable, but she didn't contradict me or blurt out the truth, so I counted it as a win.

Inside the back bedroom, Grandma LaSalle asked us a few simple questions and Gracie gave some simple answers. Something like: How's your mother doing? (Gracie: Good.) What have you been up to this summer? (Gracie: Not much. Hanging around the house.) How's your nana? (Gracie: Good, I think.) That kind of thing.

As they carried on the polite chitchat, I took in the articles that hung on the walls again. I'd needed information the last time I was here, but now there was a new urgency. Plus, I needed different information. I had to find out more about the witch and how to reverse her magic. If I could find anything about someone named Matthew, that would be icing on the cake.

One article that hung on the wall across the room from Gracie and Grandma LaSalle included a hand-drawn picture. It looked like a pencil sketch that had been reproduced in a newspaper of some kind. It showed a man in a black suit, and other people behind him, forming a crowd in front of the marsh. They carried torches and were angry, mouths open—shouting, perhaps. Only the man in black looked calm as he pointed toward the marsh. A young woman in a long dress cowered off to the side. Her hands covered her face; she was crying. A caption at the bottom read: "Miss Zofia Kowalczyk is banished from the island."

The next article included a photo that showed damage from a storm that had hit Galveston. Houses were ripped apart. Trees had fallen. Debris lined the streets. Someone had written in pen *Witch Also Causes Storm of 1915* at the bottom.

After feeling the witch's strange wind today, and her icy breath across my face, I believed it.

I stepped aside, to the next hanging item: a newspaper article whose headline was, "Witch Causes Plague; Takes Twelve Lives."

Whoa. *Plague?* I shuddered. That sounded awful. It was dated June 20, 1920, and a picture showed three men in white aprons with a pile of dead rats on a table in front of them. Yuck.

Maybe the witch could do all of this bad stuff, but these articles weren't what I needed. I circled the room until I was back by the door. The clipping I'd spotted yesterday hung there: "Witch Fires Freeze Three." My heart clenched. Witch Fires? That had to be what was overpowering Mom and Duck and Tofu. I reached up and tugged out the thumbtack.

Gracie was still chatting with Grandma LaSalle like they were old friends. "Nana might need cataract surgery too," Gracie said. "Someday. That's what her doctors said."

"Excuse me," I butted in, and I slipped the article onto the table near Mrs. LaSalle. "What was going on here? Do you know what happened?"

She picked up the paper and held it close to her face. "Ah, yes, in 1980. The witch fires froze three people. They were on Jamaica Beach, just enjoying their day, when they were suddenly frozen."

"Wow," Gracie whispered. I could tell she was trying not to give away our situation.

Good job, I thought, and I nodded at her to let her know I saw how well she was doing.

"Can you imagine?" Grandma LaSalle asked. "Being frozen for four days?"

"They were frozen for *four days*?" I sounded more worried than I should have. Dang it. Here I was, worried about Gracie giving away what had happened, and I hadn't kept my own reaction in check. "I mean," I amended, "that sounds like a long time."

"Indeed," she said. "The fire department was about to cart them off to the hospital when the fires flew off and the people could move again."

"So, um," I said, trying not to sound too excited or interested. "Why did the fires leave? Any idea? I mean, did someone get rid of them, or did the witch do something?"

"No one knows," Grandma LaSalle said.

"No one?" Gracie asked. Her voice shook. She was close to crying.

Oh Gracie, I thought.

Then again, I'd just let my emotions get the better of me too. This was tough stuff.

"Wow," I said, and I waved Gracie out of the way so I could move to stand closer to Grandma LaSalle. That way, if Gracie needed to cry, she could hide it. She took the hint and shuffled to the other side of the room, studying the papers on the wall like I had before. I could hear her sniffles as I turned back to Grandma LaSalle.

"Let's see," I said, and I pointed to a name at the bottom of the article, "this was written by someone named Marion Harris. Do you know her, by chance? She was a reporter, it looks like. Maybe she discovered what happened."

Grandma LaSalle pointed to the picture in the article. Two of the people stood in odd positions, as if they had been playing beach volleyball in the moments before being frozen. The third one was lying on the ground like perhaps they fell the moment the flame got them. Each one had a ball of fire over their heads. Grandma LaSalle put her finger on one of the people standing, the one looking away from the camera.

In her creaky voice, she said, "I don't know that reporter, but that's your nana. If anyone knows what happened and what set it right, it would be her."

Chapter Thirteen

On September the eighth, Zofia trudged across town. She and Abigail had been to lunch several times, gone for walks, and visited shops by the ocean. It had been lovely, but Zofia wasn't expecting the invitation to Abigail's seventeenth birthday party when it arrived.

Yet, here she was, on her way to the twins' house. The address on the card was 2618 Broadway Avenue J, and as she approached, she sucked in a quick breath. This house was a mansion!

The property had a massive tan brick front porch that was covered in arches. The house itself was a deep red, with gabled roofs and turrets. It was fancier than many hotels Zofia had seen, and bigger. She was intimidated, and she nearly didn't go inside, but the day was turning dark, and it looked like rain was coming, so she rang the doorbell.

Zofia's arms ached as held her spirit cabinet against her chest; she hadn't dared leave it in the boardinghouse. Someone might break into her room and take it.

When Abigail opened the door, Zofia smiled. "Happy birthday," she said.

"I'm so glad you're here," Abigail replied, and she welcomed Zofia with a warm kiss on the cheek.

"I'm sorry I'm late," Zofia said. "The walk was longer than I anticipated."

"It must have been unbearable," Abigail said. "I should have sent a carriage to get you, forgive me."

"No, no," Zofia said.

Abigail eyed the cabinet in Zofia's arms with curiosity. "May I place that somewhere for you?"

"I'll set it down inside," Zofia said.

The spirit cabinet, when placed on the floor, came to Zofia's mid-thigh. It was ordinary looking. Constructed from plain wood but lacquered nicely, with two doors and a drawer below. It held her special charmed items: an accordion, a tambourine, and a candelabra with three prongs. Of course there were secrets—concealed panels, false bottoms, masked springs, and mysterious puzzle drawers—but those were hers alone.

A boy who looked a bit younger than Abigail approached. "What do we have here?" He was eyeing the cabinet.

"It's... my prized possession," Zofia answered. She had met plenty of people who thought speaking to the dead was evil. One man in New York, in fact, had spat at her and called her a devil woman when she performed her magic show in the street. She hadn't met enough people in Galveston to know what sort of superstitious beliefs they held—or not.

The young man bent down to get closer to the spirit cabinet. "My, my," he said, and there was a hint of envy in his voice.

"Zofia, this is my brother, Matthew," Abigail said. She tapped him on his shoulder. "Really, Matthew, you could introduce yourself rather than ogle my friend's goods."

Matthew rose and offered Zofia his hand. "Forgive me. It's a pleasure to meet you, Miss..."

"Call me Zofia," Zofia said as she placed her hand in his.

He gave the softest squeeze that might qualify for a handshake. "And where have you joined us from?"

"New York City."

"New York City?" Matthew said. "I've heard it's filled with heathens."

"Oh, poppycock," Abigail said.

"Sister," he chided, "language. What if Father heard you?"

Abigail rolled her eyes. "We both know what I think of Father's rules."

"And we both know what he'll do if he catches you breaking them." He nodded at her, like the punishment would be severe.

So this family had disagreements, Zofia surmised. Perhaps small, like over the use of a word. Perhaps large.

———·———

Zofia was thrilled to find that dinner was served at this birthday party, as well as cake, and she ate as much as she thought polite.

Over coffee, one of the guests, a girl named Jane, asked Zofia if she was employed.

"Yes. I am..." She paused. "As a performer of sorts."

Jane pulled her hand to her chest. "How exciting."

Zofia looked around nervously. She hadn't told Abigail about her gift of communicating with the dead, and she wasn't sure what her friend would think. "Oh, it's nothing," she said.

"Nonsense. Tell us more," Jane said.

"I'm a spiritualist," Zofia said, steeling herself.

Jane's eyes went wide. "You lead séances?"

Abigail looked over, in her direction, and Zofia bit her lip. She knew some people didn't like such things.

In truth, Zofia hadn't offered any séances in Galveston yet. She'd only performed a few times on the boardwalk by the beach, for donations. But this could be the opportunity she needed to establish herself. She'd earned the best money in New York by offering such spectacles in the homes of rich people. There were six young ladies here in attendance, all from wealthy families. If she could pique their interest, their mothers might hire her for an engagement. Yet, she wanted to be careful.

Jane asked, "Would you be willing to show us?" There was a

conspiratorial tone to Jane's voice, as if she were suggesting Zofia break a rule or say a naughty word.

"Umm..."

Abigail said, "We'd love to see, if you wouldn't mind."

"I saw a performer in Houston who knew a man's dead wife's name without being told and even related how she died without having any connection to the family," Jane gushed.

"How fascinating." Abigail looked truly interested. She lowered her voice to ask Zofia, "Can you do something like that?"

"I'd be happy to show you," Zofia said, and she took the last sip of her coffee before a maid collected the cup. She glanced around the room. It was spacious and festive, with crepe paper strung up in celebration. "But this space isn't quite right. We need something more somber."

Abigail grabbed Zofia's hand and, leaning closer to her, said, "We can use my bedroom. It will be perfect." She waved for the friends to follow. Everyone came but Libby, who stayed behind with her coffee.

———

Zofia instructed the young ladies to gather around and stand in a circle.

Out the window, gray and black clouds hung low in the sky; it had begun to rain. A spirit approached, and through the glass, warned of a storm. It was still over the ocean but headed for Galveston. "Thank you," Zofia said softly to it. She made note that she might have to ask Abigail to spend the night if hail was on the way, or strong winds.

The other spirits came quickly when Zofia beckoned. They answered questions; they revealed secrets only the young ladies present would know. They knocked on walls and whistled. They shook the small table and brushed against the participants so that they felt a cold hand. In other words, the show was a great success.

Until a mischievous spirit entered the room. Zofia asked it to behave, but it refused. It told her it would do what it pleased. It opened all the drawers and pulled out the contents. It made things fly, cyclone-like.

Zofia panicked and shouted, "Stop, please!"

At that moment, Abigail's bedroom door flung open. There stood a man in a black suit. He looked like a fine gentleman all but for the frown on his face. "What in God's name is going on in here?" he spat. Meanwhile the items continued their flight—hairbrushes and combs and pretty hair clips. Pens and fancy stationery and pencils. And then, all at once, they dropped to the floor.

"Devil!" he gasped, and he pointed at Zofia. "Devil!" he shouted this time. "Get out of my house at once!" Zofia could see Libby standing right behind him.

Abigail stepped forward. "Don't be silly, Father. Zofia is my friend. She was conducting a séance at my request. You've heard of such things. They do them all the time in the big cities. Spiritualists—"

The man in black stepped forward and slapped Abigail across the cheek.

"It's okay," Zofia hurried to say. "I'll go."

"You can't," Abigail said, and she made a wild gesture at the windows. "The rain. Father, please."

"She will leave this house immediately," he said, and Zofia could see that he meant every word. His backbone was as straight as an arrow. His jaw was tight. He would not budge from his position.

She turned to Abigail and squeezed her hand. "It's all right," she said. "I'll go." She edged herself past Abigail's father, taking the stairs as quickly as she could.

Matthew stood near the front door. He was hovering over Zofia's spirit cabinet, her precious things. She bent down and scooped it into her arms.

Abigail's mother hurried into the hallway. "You can't go out in this weather. They say it might be a hurricane. Dear, the people from Cuba are reporting—"

But no one would hear what the people from Cuba were reporting because Abigail's father, who had followed Zofia down the stairs and into the hall, announced, "She's leaving. It is my express wish."

He pushed open the front door. It looked miserable outside. A heavy wind tore through the trees, and the rain came down in sheets.

"Father, no!" Abigail cried.

Her father stood by the door, making a shooing motion. Zofia didn't turn back to look at Abigail. She went out, into the worst hurricane to ever hit Galveston. By morning, 8,000 people would be dead.

Chapter Fourteen

Gracie and I had to get to Nana's nursing home and quickly. A car ride with Mom was out of the question, and I certainly wasn't going to try to drive or ask the LaSalles for a lift.

That left one option: we had to scooter.

Something I hated about being a twin was the lack of individuality. By that, I didn't mean that I wasn't my own person. I was. I meant that people didn't treat me that way. Me or Gracie.

Case in point: last September, when our twelfth birthday was approaching, Gracie asked for a scooter. She wanted one of those fancy electric ones. It had been some social media rage at the time, and everyone was posting pictures of themselves on their scooters. So of course Gracie had begged for one. For some reason, Mom thought it would be a great gift and bought her one, and one for me too. Even though I'd asked for new cleats and shin guards.

Gracie hadn't used the scooter much since then. The internet had moved on to something else, and the scooters looked more fun than they were in reality. They had sat in the garage all year.

But it was a good thing we had them.

The scooters were zippier than I remembered. We made a left onto Seawall Boulevard at the end of our street and took another left onto Fifty-Third. No need to get jumbled up in all the beach traffic. That's when Gracie hit the brakes. She was in front of me, and I almost crunched into her, but, luckily, I stopped in time.

"What's wrong?" I barked out.

She looked panicked. "We forgot our helmets. And our kneepads. And our elbow pads! Lana, we have to go home and get them."

Was she serious?

"Gracie, we can't go back," I said. "We have to get to Nana's."

"But—safety," she said in a high-pitched, anxious voice.

"Are you serious?" I nearly yelled. "We have to think about Mom and Duck and Tofu."

I started my scooter again and zoomed off, hoping she'd follow my lead. She did. Soon enough, we were cruising toward downtown, which was filled with square buildings and statues and parks and businesses. We took a hard right onto Broadway Avenue J and then another right onto a small street, and there was Nana's nursing home. Perfect.

We pulled the scooters over in Stoney Brook's parking lot and I made a beeline for the front door. Gracie, though, hung back. She futzed with the kickstand even though it was a simple put-it-down-and-walk-away kind of deal. She was obviously dawdling.

"Hey," I said, turning back to her, "everything okay with that kickstand?"

She pushed it into place and looked up to study the sturdy buildings across the street. "I just… I just…"

This dillydallying was getting on my nerves. "Spit it out, Gracie. You have something to say?"

Her face got red and crinkly, like she was embarrassed. "I just was wondering why you went into the marsh. I mean, everyone's always told us not to bother that witch. Why do it? Out of boredom?"

Not a bad guess, really, but not quite right. I realized no flip answer would do. She deserved the truth since she was stuck in this situation with me. I tugged the key out from under my shirt and held it out for Gracie to see.

"Oh, that's Da—" She cut herself off, swallowed, and said, "That was...his."

Dad's. She still wouldn't talk about him, but she knew this key. Interesting.

"Yeah," I said. "How did you know that?"

"He used to wear it around his neck, just like you have it. I haven't seen it in years." She sniffed and wiped a hand across the bottom of her nose.

"He used to wear this?" I couldn't believe it.

"He did." Gracie grimaced like she was on the brink of strong emotions. Oh boy. But she held it together. She said, "I remember this one time when we were little—like five or something—I was sitting on his lap, and I saw a bit of that blue." She pointed to the ribbon around my neck. "I asked him what it was, and he pulled out that key."

My heart skipped a beat. "What did he say? What was it about? Why did he wear it?" I was talking a mile a minute. Fine. This was urgent.

She shrugged. "I have no idea. He just said it was a key and he let me touch it and then he tucked it back under his shirt."

"And?" I pressed. "And?"

Gracie waved her arms like she was frustrated and didn't know what to say. "What? I was like five, Lana. I didn't interrogate him about it, okay?"

"Yeah, okay," I said, and I shook my head to try to take in this information.

- Dad had had this key for a while—since we were five at least.
- He wasn't trying to hide it. He'd shown it to Gracie.

But it must have to do with the witch somehow or it wouldn't have been in that envelope with the note.

"Where did you find it?" Gracie asked.

"In an envelope," I said, and I pulled it out of my back pocket. (Had I removed Dad's stuff from my mud-covered shorts and put it in the clean pair I now had on? You betcha.) "This note was inside." As Gracie read, she made little gasping noises that reminded me of a fish out of water. "It sounded to me like he had a job to do. Something he didn't get to do before he died. Something to do with the witch. So, I wanted to help. I wanted, I don't know, to do it for him or something. You know, remember him."

"That's why you went to see the witch."

"That's why I went."

Gracie nodded and stared at the note. "Did you ask the witch about the key?"

"I did, and instead of answering me, she cursed our family."

Gracie whispered something under her breath that I couldn't quite make out. It couldn't have been a swear word; she didn't swear, ever. But it sure sounded like one.

"Anyway, that's what happened," I summed up.

Gracie nodded, refolded the note, tucked it in the envelope, and grimaced.

"Hopefully Nana can help us fix the witch fires," I said. I took the envelope from Gracie and returned it to my back pocket. "We might have to forget about what Dad was or wasn't going to do for now."

"Yeah," she said. Then she jolted, as if remembering something. "Nana's going to kill you." She sounded as earnest as she ever had.

"Nana? She might." In fact, she would. Absolutely. Nana would Kill me with a capital *K* if she knew I'd gone to see that witch. She

84

would drag me through the mud (metaphorically speaking), then she would yell at me (also metaphorically speaking, since she couldn't yell right now; she could only write in capital letters), then she would get me grounded (not metaphorically speaking. She'd have Mom on her side in a heartbeat. That was, once Mom was unfrozen.). Nana had always told us to stay away from that witch. I would be in big, big, big trouble if I had to tell her this was all because of me. Because I went into the marsh and bothered the witch.

Gracie shook her head. "She's going to kill you, kill you."

"Point taken," I said, "but she will only want to kill me if she *knows*." I watched Gracie for a reaction but didn't get one. I'd have to be more direct. "What do you think about keeping it quiet that I was the one who went into the marsh and bothered the witch?"

Gracie stayed silent, staring back at me.

"I'm not suggesting we lie," I went on, trying to win her over, "just withhold all the information until later. What do you say?" Her eyebrows got bunchy. She was considering it. "I can totally get in trouble later," I added. "But maybe we could just handle the whole flame thing first. What do you think?"

She hesitated, and then she looked me straight in the eye. "It can be our secret," she said. "For now."

"Really?" Never in a million years would I have thought Gracie would do this for me. Then again, she had let me lie to the LaSalles.

Well, good. Maybe Gracie was changing.

Gracie said in total deadpan, "I wouldn't want to have to tell Nana that I went over the fence either."

"Thanks."

"But Lana," she said, "we'll have to tell her eventually."

"Of course." I hurried to the front door of that nursing home and flung it open. "After you."

Ms. Doris, the front desk lady, sat at her normal post. We'd met her when Nana moved in. She waved at us and buzzed us in.

"Ah, the Parker girls," she said when we entered the lobby.

Sigh. We were always the Parker girls or the Parker twins or Amelie's twins.

"Remind me of your names," she said.

At least she remembered we had individual names.

She pointed at me. "Is it Gracie?"

I shook my head. "I'm Lana."

"Ah," she said, "then, you're Gracie," and here she gestured to Gracie.

Gracie and I didn't look alike, but once people found out we were twins, they couldn't tell us apart. We were lumped together. It was like their brains said, "Twins look the same," and so they got us mixed up, even though our family resemblance was slim at best.

Granted, Ms. Doris didn't know us well. I wasn't really blaming her. On the other hand, it happened waaaay too much.

"Right," I said. "I'm Lana and that's Gracie. We're here to see our nana."

Ms. Doris smiled and nodded.

I leaned over the counter, creating a kind of secret sleuth vibe. "Any progress on the talking thing?"

She frowned and shook her head. "Sorry, dear. But your nana can walk like a pro and yesterday she played catch with the physical therapist."

"Wow," I went to say. But Gracie butted in. "That's great news. I miss her a lot."

Ms. Doris gave Gracie a smile. "I know she's missed you too. Clem will be happy to see you."

Clem was short for Clementine. Dad's side of the family—as they used to say—they were American as pie. Or oranges, in this case.

Ms. Doris nodded toward the long hallway at the end of the lobby, which was her way of telling us we were free to go. We thanked her, then headed on our way.

The closer we got to Nana's room, the gloomier Gracie seemed. I wondered if being here reminded her of better times, normal times. Nana taking us to the Galveston Fair and Rodeo. Nana telling us funny stories about her bowling team. Nana bringing over jelly donuts on Hanukkah even though we aren't Jewish.

I missed those times too.

When we reached room 606, we stood in front of the door for a good minute, each of us anticipating what was to come. Finally, I said, "I guess let's go." Gracie knocked and opened the door.

Nana was sitting at her small kitchen table, eating lunch.

We stepped inside. "Hi, Nana." Gracie and I said this at the same time.

Not cool. And no, it wasn't a twin moment. Just a coincidence.

Nana got up, wiped her mouth on a napkin, and came toward us. She held out her arms. I knew what this meant. Gracie and I were expected to both hug her. Together. Another twin thing. But this wasn't the time for complaining. This was the time for giving Nana a you're-doing-great squeeze. I squished in next to Gracie and held them both tight.

Nana's hair used to be the same color as mine (I'd seen pictures), but it had turned white back before I was born. Her eyes were the same color as Dad's. At least, that's what I used to think. Now, I couldn't really remember. Little details about Dad escaped with each passing month. They slipped away, like if you tossed a paper airplane up and it caught the wind. He had turned into a fuzzy image in my head, and I had to look at a picture to remember all his features. But right after he died, I saw Nana and I thought her eyes looked just like his, so I held on to that. The same blue with darker green streaks. Even then, I knew to hang on to that.

When Nana let us go, she gestured for us to sit in the part of her small space that was supposed to be a living room. She had two chairs and a two-seater couch, so it worked.

"Do you want to finish your lunch first?" I asked.

She made a motion like she was done anyway, and we sat down. Nana and Gracie took the two-seater couch. I plunked into a chair.

There were a bunch of small weights on the floor, like she'd been exercising.

"You've been working hard," I said to Nana, gesturing at the weights.

She nodded and half her face smiled, looking proud.

Well, she should have felt proud.

"And no more walker. Great. That's just great." I swallowed. Enough small talk. I had to get to the point. "Nana," I said, taking a serious tone, "we came to ask you about the Alligator Witch."

One side of Nana's face turned into storm clouds, and she sat up like if she was able to talk, she might give me a whole lecture on the subject. She moved her hands in a way that suggested, *I've warned you about her for years.*

"So you believe in her," I said, which was silly, really. Anyone who'd been frozen by witch fires would believe in her, but this was my bridge into the subject.

Nana nodded gravely.

"Okay, great, because I need to know something," I continued. "Mrs. LaSalle—the older one—she showed me an old newspaper article when I was at her house. There was a picture of three people, and they had flames over their heads. They were frozen." I watched Nana for a reaction, but she held stoically still. "She said one of them was you."

Nana made a grunting noise and squirmed in her seat.

"Can you tell us about what happened?" I asked.

She squirmed some more, and moved her mouth as if she wished she could say something.

"I heard that three people were frozen in 1980 and that witch fires held them in place for four days."

Nana nodded. I was on the right track.

But then, Gracie shot out, "Mom and Duck are frozen!"

Nana gasped and kind of crumpled into the couch.

Oh Gracie. She hadn't blurted to Nancy, and she hadn't blurted to the LaSalles. I guessed it was just time. There was only so long goody-two-shoes Gracie could hold in a secret like that. Maybe it was better this way. Nana would know why I was asking about the witch; she would understand the stakes involved. I just had to keep Nana positive and focused and Gracie not falling apart.

I could do it. Or, I hoped I could.

I had to try.

"It's true," I said, trying to convey a sense of calm. "But we think you can help us," I told Nana. "We need to know how the witch fires were put out back in 1980. Can you do that for us, Nana? Can you tell us what happened?"

Nana looked unsure. Then she let out a sob that was so loud and watery, I wondered if her neighbors would hear and worry.

This was not good. It wasn't just Nana at stake here. Gracie always cried when someone else cried. Even if that someone else was on TV or in a movie.

I leaned close to Nana and laid what I hoped was a comforting hand on her shoulder, and while I did that, I snuck a glance at Gracie. No waterworks yet, thank goodness, but they were coming. I rubbed Nana's shoulder and said "It's important" in the most soothing voice I could. "We need your help. We really need to know what happened."

"Please," Gracie said, and she started sputtering. Oh no. "We need—what if Mom never comes out of it?"

And then she was sobbing.

And so was Nana. And then they were hugging each other and crying harder.

But it didn't seem to bother Gracie. She was squeezed on that couch next to Nana and she hugged her tight, and they both had a good cry. Or, I hoped it was a good cry.

When they were ready to mop up their faces, I handed them tissues. Five for Gracie. Five for Nana. One more for Gracie. One more for Nana. I held my breath.

Their eyes were red, and their cheeks were wet and blotchy, but they were calming down.

"Thanks," Gracie squeaked at me. I think she meant for the tissues. She blew her nose and then said, "Nana, I've missed you." Her voice was low and scratchy. "I haven't come visit because...because..."

Nana nodded and wiped the tears that kept springing from the corners of her eyes. She patted Gracie's knee like she knew what Gracie was going to say.

Gracie went on, "Because it was so hard to see you... not doing well."

Nana patted Gracie again, but this time in a way that communicated *It's okay, I understand.*

I grew restless. This crying and bonding and forgiving was fine, but we had a mission to accomplish, a mystery to solve, and it was important. "She forgives you," I said to Gracie. "Can we handle the whole witch fire thing now?"

Was I being impatient and near rude? Sure, but Nana and Gracie didn't let it bother them. Nana took Gracie's face in her hands and gave her a lopsided kiss on her cheek.

"Thanks," Gracie whispered.

"Really, this is great," I said. "But Mom and Duck and Tofu are frozen, and we need to figure out how to unfreeze them."

Nana nodded and stood up, looking surprisingly agile. She threw out the used tissues, and returned to that small kitchen table, where she pushed aside the lunch things and picked up a notepad and pen. Gripping them, she narrowed her eyes like she was thinking. She wrote something, and then flashed the paper at us: PAPA GOT A... THING... AND THE FIRES WENT OUT.

"Great," I said. "What was it? What was that thing?"

Nana turned the notepad back to face her again and tapped the pen against it, like she was thinking, thinking. She squinted her eyes even more. She shook her head; she was obviously trying to come up with a word but couldn't. She grunted an angry grunt.

"It's okay, Nana," Gracie said. "I forget words all the time too."

Not true, but it was a nice thing to say.

Gracie gave me a nudge. "Yeah, me too," I lied.

Nana grew more frustrated, but then she seemed to come up

with an idea. She put the notepad and pen down and motioned for us to watch. Okay, we were watching. She moved her right hand in a waving motion out and in—moving toward the center of her body and then back out again. Her left one she held up but only swayed slightly.

"Um...," I said. I had no clue what she was going for. When I turned to Gracie, she shrugged like she didn't know either.

Nana kept on with that motion, adding a hum to go along with it.

Baffling.

"Sorry, Nana," I said.

"Clapping?" Gracie guessed. "Beating a drum? Cymbals?"

Nana shook her head and sighed. She wrote IT'S AN INSTRUMENT on her notepad.

"Flute? Clarinet?" I ventured, but Nana looked hopeless. Gracie and I had both managed to avoid music lessons. We weren't going to get far with these guesses.

Then, Nana seemed to remember something and jaunted into the other room—her bedroom. When she reappeared, she held a cardboard box and made a noise like *humm, hooom* as if she wanted our attention.

Well, she had it. Oh, yes, she had it.

Nana settled the box onto the coffee table and blew across its top. Dust specks went flying. Gracie and I both cringed, but the dust didn't seem to bother Nana. She was opening up the box and making those *humm, hoom* noises again. She brought stuff out—all kinds of stuff. A framed... something. Not a picture. It had words on it. A black billowy thing. Maybe some kind of robe? A funny black hat. Flat and square. Then came the pictures. Photo albums and frames and a big scrapbook. She paused at the bottom and pulled out a book-like object. She seemed to want to handle this one with care, and I could see why. It had a yellow cover, discolored with age.

Nana gestured at us to make room on the small table near the couch, and then she placed the book down. It was another scrapbook. On the front, it said, EARLY YEARS OF MATRIMONY. She flipped through it, turning each page only after searching through the photos, words, and small bits of paper that were taped down. About halfway through, her right eyebrow furrowed and half her face grimaced. The further into the scrapbook she got, the deeper that grimace grew. When she reached the end, she sighed and closed the scrapbook. She scooped up that notepad again and wrote, *THERE'S A PICTURE OF THE...THING, BUT NOT HERE*. Once we'd read it, she added, *WE NEED TO GET TO MY HOUSE*.

"Um," I said, "are you sure? Nothing's in your house except the board games and a few pieces of furniture. Most of your stuff is... well, not there anymore."

WHERE IS IT? Nana wrote.

"Storage," I said. "But it's a nice unit. Air-conditioned." Mom had told me that much.

"Yeah," Gracie said. "I've been there; it's great. We're all hoping you can return home soon, Nana, and as soon as you can, we'll get your stuff back in your house." Her voice came out more like she was trying to sound upbeat than really believing it.

Nana shook her head and looked sad, but a moment later, she went to her hall closet and got out a bright pink fanny pack, which she strapped on. She tucked a few things from the kitchen table in it. Then, she was ready.

WE'VE GOT TO GO TO THE STORAGE PLACE, she wrote before tucking the notepad into her fanny pack and zipping it shut. She looked at us like she was daring us to say no.

We didn't. We wouldn't. We knew better. You didn't cross Nana. She was—what's the phrase? A formidable woman.

So, a field trip was in the works and Nana was taking the lead.

Chapter Fifteen

When we walked out of Nana's room, I turned toward the lobby and the front door, but Nana pulled me to a stop. She shook her head.

"What is it?" Gracie asked.

Nana took out that notepad and wrote, THEY WON'T LET ME GO.

"Who won't let you go?" I asked.

NURSING HOME PEOPLE WON'T LET ME LEAVE. NOT WITHOUT "ADULT SUPERVISION."

The quotes around *adult supervision* told me this frustrated Nana. She felt capable, and she *was* capable now, but it didn't matter. "You're sure?" I asked. "Maybe we should ask."

THEY WON'T LET ME GO UNLESS YOUR MOM IS HERE.

Well, there was little chance of that.

"What are we going to do?" Gracie said with a moan. She looked sad and small and scared.

Nana held her chin high and stamped her foot. SNEAK, she wrote.

Then she pivoted, going down the hall in the opposite direction with speed I didn't know she had. Nana stopped by a door three down from hers and knocked. She wrote something on her notepad and showed it to the woman who answered.

The woman was ancient looking in a classic old lady kind of way. Her face was a mask of wrinkles, and she was shorter than me, which was saying something. Slippers on her feet. Red velvet tracksuit.

A knot of silver hair piled onto the top of her head. She wore a pair of dark sunglasses even though we were inside. She lifted them to read Nana's note and then said in a gritty voice, "Certainly, Clem. Right this way." She ushered us inside her room.

Gracie and I paused in the entryway, but Nana went in as if she'd been inside a million times. She hurried straight through the living room area and rushed through the door that led to the bedroom. I heard something that sounded like a sliding glass door and dashed after her.

The bedroom had a little balcony that overlooked the side lawn. Nana was already outside, gripping the rail like she was going to climb over.

"Whoa, whoa," I cried. I sprinted over and grabbed her arm before she could vault to her death. "Nana. Whatcha up to?" The balcony was close to the ground, but still.

She pointed to the grass. Yup, her plan was to lumber over the rail and escape.

"I know you've been going to physical therapy and lifting weights," I said, "but I can't have you breaking a leg. I need your help. A trip to the ER would gum up the works."

Nana made noises and looked offended. Out came that notepad again. *CAN DO IT*, she wrote.

Gracie appeared on the balcony too, and I waited for a second while she surveyed the scene before asking, "What do you think?"

She stepped closer to the rail and gazed down. Then she sized up Nana. Nana stood taller, like she was trying to prove to Gracie that she could do it.

"Let me go first," Gracie said. It was a kind of concession. "I'll see how hard it is."

Nana wasn't buying it. She waved her hands at Gracie and stomped her feet and gave her a half face filled with self-righteousness.

Gracie said, "I'm not saying you can't do it. I just want to be there at the bottom to steady you if you need help."

Nana threw her two hands on her hips.

"Not catch you," Gracie said. "And for the record, I don't think you'll need me. Just being cautious." Anyone who knew Gracie knew she played it safe, so this was believable.

"No broken legs," I said. "That's going to be one of our rules today."

Nana pouted but nodded her assent.

Gracie vaulted over the rail onto the grass without trouble. She held out her arms, but Nana didn't need her help. She landed just fine.

"Thank you so much, ma'am," I said to the tracksuit woman, who watched us from inside her bedroom.

"If that Doris comes looking, I'll tell her we're visiting," she called out to Nana. "But be back by dinner. I can't help if the nurse who doles out evening meds can't find you."

Nana nodded and waved, like of course she'd be back by then and, after I got down, we headed across the lawn, toward the parking lot.

"That was some escape," I said to Nana.

She beamed back at me with half a smile.

But when we reached the scooters, we ran into trouble.

"Come on, Nana," I said. "I'll steer. All you have to do is hold on to me."

In some kind of rebellious rebuttal, she climbed onto my scooter and gripped the handlebars. She glanced at me, and then behind her, like I should go there.

"Nana," I said.

Nana disembarked and, tugging the notepad out of her fanny pack, wrote, *I NEED TO HOLD ON TO THE HANDLEBARS FOR BALANCE.*

"Do you know how to work this?" I asked. It was one thing to ride a bike, and a completely different thing to drive an electric scooter.

Nana made a distinct *easy peasy* gesture.

"Fine," I said, resigned. "Let's go." I called to Gracie, "Do you know where the storage place is?"

"Yeah," she said. "Not far." She was on her phone again, so I guessed she had looked up directions.

"We'll follow you."

The next few minutes were—in one word—scary.

They involved a lot of Gracie turning around, only to see us right on her tail, and then speeding up, with Nana zooming along to stay close. When Nana whipped around corners, I had to lean far to the opposite side to keep the scooter upright.

And when we arrived at the storage place, I thought for sure Nana would ram right into the front door. She stopped *just* in the nick of time.

That woman was a menace, I'll tell you what.

In the storage place's parking lot, Gracie got off her scooter and gave me a wide-eyed stare, like she had never been so scared in her life. I held my stomach, afraid I might puke.

Nana only snapped the fingers on her right hand as if wanting our attention and waved us forward. We followed. The worst had to be over, right?

Chapter Sixteen

The front gate of the place, called appropriately U-STORE-IT, was locked. There was a keypad, which I stared closely at. "Do you know the code?" I asked Gracie.

She shook her head. "Mom always did it."

"Guess we're going to have to find someone who works here," I said.

We made our way to the front, following signs for the office, and trucked inside. A guy was sitting at a desk eating from a bag of chips and watching sports on his phone. He clicked it off when he saw us. "Sorry, sorry," he said. "Just grabbing an afternoon snack. Didn't hear you come up."

"No worries, sir," I said. I figured I'd better take the lead on this. "We need to get into my nana's storage unit, but we forgot the code for the front gate."

"It happens," he said, and he produced a napkin from somewhere and wiped his mouth. "I'll let you in."

"Thank you so much." I gave Nana and Gracie a big smile because this was going great. We'd have whatever Nana needed in a second or two.

The man led us outside, back the way we'd come, and he tapped in the code. "Which unit are you looking for?" he asked.

I wanted to curse right then and there because I had no idea. "Oh, we'll know it when we see it," I said breezily.

"Not likely," he said with a shake of his head. "We have over two hundred units." He scratched the skin under his chin. "Do you have a double or a deluxe?"

"Um...," I started.

He pointed to the left. "The double units are that way, numbers one to one-hundred-and-sixty, and"—here he pointed to the right—"the deluxe units are over there. Numbers one-sixty-one to two-hundred-twenty." He rubbed under his chin again. "I sure hope you have one of those because the others are un-air-conditioned and phew!" He blew out a blubbery breath. "It's a hot one today!"

"It sure is," I said, my heart sinking.

"Thanks, sir," Gracie butted in. "It's number two-hundred-and-twelve. I know where it is."

"Wonderful," he said. "I'm glad to hear that," and he waved his arm toward the now-opened gate like he was a king allowing us entrance.

At least Gracie knew where we were going.

We scooted inside.

"Thanks!" I called over my shoulder. Softly, to Gracie, I said, "I'm glad you knew the unit."

"Yeah, well, I helped Mom with the last load of stuff."

She sounded... what? Annoyed, maybe? Frustrated? Sure, I hadn't helped. I remembered the day—I had found a bunch of soccer videos online, so I offered to stay home and watch Duck instead of joining. But I'd been useful.

"You really came through there knowing the number is all I'm saying," I said.

"Oh no, oh no," Gracie moaned as we reached unit 212, which was secured by a combination lock.

"What's wrong?" I asked.

"I don't know how to open this lock," she said, her breath coming out heavy. "Mom always did this one too." She spun the numerical dials to random numbers and pulled on the device. It didn't budge. She tried again.

"Okay," I said, and I put out a hand to stop her arbitrary spinning. "It's okay."

"It's not!" Gracie exclaimed.

"Let's just take a minute to think about this." I squeezed her upper arm, and she took her hands off the lock. "Mom brought the lock, right?"

"I think so," Gracie said in a small voice.

"Good. We can figure this out." I studied the dials. Four numbers. That's the code we were looking for. "We need a four-digit combination," I said.

"It could be anything." Gracie held her head in her hands. "How many possible combinations are there?"

"Thousands," I said. "Maybe hundreds of thousands. But we're not going to make random guesses. Hold on."

My brain clunked along, and I wished it would move faster, but the sun was beating down on us and Nana was looking anxious, and Gracie was starting to hyperventilate.

"If Mom brought this lock with her, then the combination is probably something she set herself. Something she could remember. It can't be that hard." And then, it came to me. They always said you weren't supposed to use your birthday for things like this. But what if Mom had? She was an English teacher; technical issues weren't really her thing. Besides, it was just a lock at a storage place. Who would know her birthday? I spun the dials to her birthday, which was in December, and then I pulled down on the lock.

Nothing. It didn't open.

"What did you try?" Gracie asked.

"Mom's birthday."

"Try Duck's," she suggested.

I spun the dials again to a date in April. Nope. I shook my head.

"Do Dad's."

I was surprised to hear Gracie say the word *Dad* but I didn't want to make a big deal of it. "Sure."

Gracie stood with her head hanging over my shoulder, watching me. She was so invested I might have heard her heart thumping in anticipation.

I put in the numbers and pulled.

Nothing. The lock stayed stuck. "This is hopeless," I said. It might have been Gracie's head hanging so close over my shoulder, or the heat of the sun getting the best of me, or the whole terrible situation. I was at the end of my rope. "Dang it!" I swung the lock hard, harder than I meant to. It clanged against the metal door, and I stomped away.

Gracie followed me and, after giving me the time to huff out three big breaths, she laid a hand on my shoulder. "It's okay," she said. "We'll get it." She was so calm. I let out another huff.

That's when Nana made a noise of triumph. Gracie and I spun around. Nana gestured at the open lock with a sound that was surprisingly close to "Ta-da!"

"Nana, you're a genius!" Gracie squealed. "How'd you do it? What was the combo?"

Nana wrote out a date on her notepad. Our birthday.

"Well who would have thought?" I said with a half chuckle.

"Almost you," Gracie said, and she patted my shoulder. "You got the birthday thing right."

"I guess so," I admitted. "Let's go."

Gracie and I rushed to the metal door and pushed it up. We nearly barreled through.

Nana, though, didn't follow us. She stood in the open doorway, even though there was AC blowing inside.

I went back for her. "Come on, Nana." But although I held out my hand for her, she didn't move. She didn't reach out for me, and she didn't take a step in. She wrapped her arms around herself.

"What's wrong?" I asked.

With shaking hands, she got that notepad again. *ALL MY THINGS*, she wrote. *MY WHOLE LIFE.*

It was her life—boxed up and carted away from where it should have been.

"Things will be back to normal before you know it," I said, and I nodded like I meant it. I wasn't sure if it was true, but I wanted it to be.

She squared her shoulders like she was trying hard to believe it too, and strutted into the unit. *WE'RE LOOKING FOR AN OLIVE-GREEN TRUNK*, she wrote.

Way to go, Nana.

"Olive-green trunk. On it," I said as I pushed farther inside. There were cardboard boxes everywhere. Nana's furniture. Her clothes. Her things.

I opened drawers (just in case). I looked under tables and got behind big stacks of stuff to inspect behind them (again, just in case). I studied shelves and boxes big enough to hold a trunk. Where could it be? I was starting to lose hope when Gracie called, "We've got it."

I made my way back to the front of the unit, where Gracie and Nana were. As I went, I bumped my hip on a small end table. A card from a board game sat on top of it—One Night Ultimate Werewolf. I scooped it up. "Hey," I said, coming toward Nana and Gracie, "look what I found." I turned the card so they could see the picture on the front. It showed a woman with big eyes. "Looks like I'm the insomniac."

Nana smiled. She curled her fingers like claws and grabbed at me like she was a werewolf and made a noise close to a growl.

"That's right," I said, ducking away from her outstretched hands. "Your strategy for winning every time," and I laughed because when we first played this game, it seemed like Nana didn't understand what to do or how to play. In the game, everyone got a secret card that revealed their game identities—like the insomniac woman. One person was always the werewolf and if you were the werewolf, you had to convince the other players that you weren't. You played innocent—like "I'm just a nice, unsuspecting villager," or "I'm just the town doctor," or "I was up all night because I have trouble sleeping."

But Nana pretended to be the werewolf every time. We'd start the questioning round, and she'd butt in: "Rarr!" Every time. It turned out to be a decent strategy. Because she always pretended to be the werewolf, we never actually thought she was. She won most rounds.

I laid the card down, though, because we had to stay focused. We had to save Mom and Duck and Tofu. "No time like the present," I declared. "Let's crack that bad boy open."

The olive-green trunk was big and already opened, actually.

Nana started lifting things out; Gracie and I helped. There were a lot of books and old photos.

Then, Nana gasped. She scooped up an old journal and started flipping through it until she pointed at a page, looking triumphant. There was a bunch of writing, but what jumped out to me was an old photo. It was a Polaroid and so ancient that the colors were fading and there was a crack running up the side. The picture showed an accordion that was silver and red with black handles. A message was handwritten across the bottom of the photo: *In the Odds and Ends Antique Shop, I found what I needed.*

Nana pointed at the accordion with gusto, like it was important.

"*Accordion*," I said. "An accordion."

Nana nodded.

Gracie shook her head. "We should have known. Sorry, Nana."

It seemed obvious now. Nana had been trying to move her hands like she was playing an accordion. The stroke had limited her motion on the left, though.

"Yeah, sorry, Nana," I said, "but at least we got it now." I leaned closer. This picture was important. No, the accordion was! It was more than important! It had belonged to the witch. Yes, it was the exact instrument I had seen this morning! "So Papa got this. He found it at an antique shop, and it made the witch fires go out, right?" I asked. "Did he return it to the witch?" My voice came out breathy. It made sense. The witch had told me to *return what was hers*. Papa had found this accordion, and he must have somehow known it belonged to the Alligator Witch, and returned it, and then the flames had vanished. That must be it.

Nana nodded.

"Okay, great." I felt like we were cooking with gas now. "So returning the witch's accordion saved you. We just need to find something else that belonged to her. Something that was taken or stolen or just isn't with her anymore."

"How are we going to do that?" Gracie asked.

"Easy," I said, and I gently pulled the Polaroid out of the journal. "If Papa found what he needed at the Odds and Ends Antique Shop, then we should start there." I tugged out my phone. "Maybe there's a Matthew who works there."

"You think that shop still exists?" Gracie asked. "Papa went there in 1980." She said this like it was the dawn of time.

She had a point.

"Might as well look," I said, and I started typing in a search.

Nana stopped me by placing her hand on mine. She nodded then shook her head, then nodded again. Dang it, this pantomime had me confused.

"What are you trying to say?" I asked.

That notepad came out. *THE STRAND*, she wrote.

"Odds and Ends was a shop in the Strand?"

She wrote: *IS*.

"Well then, what are we waiting for? Let's roll like a donut hole!"

Chapter Seventeen
ZOFIA, 1900

The night of the storm was the worst night of Zofia's life.

She tried to make it back home, to the boardinghouse, but it was impossible. Rain lashed, feeling like steel spikes were driving into her skin. The wind blew so hard, her breath was sucked from her lungs. Water covered the street, rising and rising. Zofia couldn't take another step with her dress dragging behind her. And then her foot slipped. She was falling!

No. She righted herself, breathing hard. There was something in front of her. Large and tall. If only she could make it there, Zofia thought, she would be okay.

She pushed herself, and after what felt like hours, she reached the structure. It was a monument, the one that stood in the town square. Zofia struggled to find something to hold on to, to pull herself up, while carrying the spirit cabinet. Finally, she managed to shimmy her body up the monument, wedging herself and her cabinet in at the top, where she barely stayed above the storm surge. Zofia clung for dear life hour after hour as the rough ocean came ashore. She heard shouts and cries and the terrible sounds of roofs being ripped off, of walls being torn apart, of houses being completely destroyed.

Now, the sun was rising; floodwater still covered the island, but it was receding. Whereas last night it had been a massive river running through town, now it was a handful of streams meandering down broken streets, headed back to the sea.

There were dead bodies everywhere—in the rubble, lying on lawns, stuck in brush—and their spirits often stayed close by. Some hung in the air, weeping into their hands. Others yelled at the sky. Others seemed not to know they were dead; they searched the wreckage for loved ones.

As Zofia scrambled down the monument, one hand around her cabinet, she noticed an alligator, stuck beneath debris piled up at the monument's base. It growled in displeasure.

"Poor thing," she said. "I'll do my best to free you, but I would prefer you not attack me once you're out."

Zofia grunted with effort as she began loosening wooden planks and what looked like the majority of a sofa from atop the alligator. The animal thrashed and squirmed in its confinement but was able to wiggle itself free eventually. It scurried off, half swimming, half limping.

"Be safe," Zofia called after it.

Its swishing tail was the only response she got.

The island was demolished. Buildings flattened. Neighborhoods reduced to piles of shredded lumber. Cars overturned and railroad train cars far from where they should be on the tracks.

But then she saw the Getty Mansion. It was standing. The roof was intact. The walls were seemingly untouched. It was a miracle. She decided to return; what other option did she have?

Her spirit cabinet clasped to her chest, Zofia made her way down the waterlogged street. Her boots sank deep in the mud, but she was glad to have them on as fragments of nails, shards of glass, and pieces of rubble covered every surface. As she got closer, she saw the Getty family. They were outside, surveying the damage around them, looking as scared and helpless as she felt. She raised a hand and called, "Abigail!"

The family turned to look at her.

Immediately, Abigail's father stomped in her direction; he looked ready to tear Zofia limb from limb. "Look at what you have done!" he shouted. "Your black magic brought this destruction to all of us. You made this storm.

You brought this hurricane!" Close to her now, he brought his hand up as if he would hit her.

Abigail, who had followed him, grabbed his arm, and stopped the blow from coming. "No, Father! Zofia did nothing. Hurricanes are a fact of nature, of science!"

"Enough," he said, turning on his daughter. "I know evil when I see it. And this girl"—he pointed at Zofia—"is evil."

He grabbed Zofia and pulled her into the house.

"You brought that storm on us!" he cried as he marched Zofia through the front hall. "All that water!" He looked like he was close to crying, but if there were tears in his eyes, they were angry ones. "Destruction everywhere. Houses are just... gone. Our neighbors. Our friends."

Zofia knew how bad it had been. She had witnessed it all and the weight of the memories felt like they would choke her.

"You have done this, you... you witch." Mr. Getty's voice had a sudden calm to it.

Abigail stood in the front door, shaking her head. "Papa, no."

"I shall have to deal with you myself," Mr. Getty said, his eyes narrowed into slits.

Zofia wanted to shove the spirit cabinet in Abigail's arms and ask her to keep it safe though she didn't dare. If she knew men like Mr. Getty (and she did), she knew that he would destroy what she loved to spite her. Best to simply stay quiet. She set it down on the marble floor of the grand foyer and hoped it would remain untouched.

Mr. Getty seized Zofia again and dragged her deeper into the mansion, to a closet off the parlor. He threw her in and locked the door. Zofia could hear Abigail crying, trying to reason with her angry father, but it was no use. Zofia stayed in the dark closet, sprawled on the floor in her soaked clothing, for hours.

When the door opened again, it was Mr. Getty, carrying a torch. He grasped Zofia by the collar and yanked her toward the front door. Outside, it was dark. Mr. Getty hauled Zofia down the long porch stairs, and there, at the bottom, a crowd waited. Men, mostly, and they looked angry. They held torches too and flaunted knives and rifles. Zofia's heart stopped, skipped a beat, and then started again.

"Burn the witch," one of the men cried. "Kill the witch!"

She wasn't a witch, she wanted to scream; she was only a spiritualist. Didn't these people know about spiritualism? Their chant suggested no, they didn't. And who knew what Mr. Getty had told them.

The men marched her, shivering, through the ruined, muddy streets of Galveston. When a large marsh was in sight, they stopped. Wood had been piled up into what could only be called a pyre. A tall tree trunk sat nestled in its middle.

The crowd chanted, "Burn the witch, burn the witch, burn the witch!"

"No!" Zofia screamed, finally letting go of her notion to remain silent. "I did nothing!"

Through the voices, Zofia could hear her friend Abigail. She was shouting, proclaiming Zofia's innocence.

No one listened.

Libby was there too, with her chin held high and her arms crossed. Zofia caught sight of their brother Matthew. He had her spirit cabinet clutched in his arms like it belonged to him.

Oh, how she longed to hold her precious instruments again, to take out the candelabra and ask it to light. She wished to call her accordion to come to her, but she knew that would only make the situation worse. These people already thought her magic was evil.

The crowd's chanting got louder. "Burn the witch! Burn the witch!"

Mr. Getty stepped forward. "We will burn you at the stake, Witch."

Zofia didn't answer because it didn't seem like a question.

He surveyed the crowd as if testing their desires. "Or," he said, "you can go. Leave forever. Leave this town in peace."

Was he suggesting that she walk into the marsh? Nothing was beyond it but the bay. Should she try to swim miles and miles to the other side—in her dress? In her boots? Or was he letting her choose the means to her own death—by fire or water? Burn at the stake or drown.

There was no good choice.

A shadow descended and swirled around the crowd, over the crowd, through the crowd. Zofia felt it at once and it made her skin prickle. The men, still chanting and yelling, were slower to notice its presence, but as it passed by, over, or through them, their yelling grew in pitch.

It wasn't a spirit or a ghost—that was, it had never been human. It resided purely in the spiritual realm. She had never encountered such a thing. It wasn't solid. Its form stayed constant... somehow... but it appeared to be made up of a thousand black dots—like a swarm of gnats. They swirled and whirled and somehow worked together.

The thing said, "It doesn't have to be this way."

"What do you mean?" Zofia squeaked out.

Mr. Getty said, "I mean that you should g—" right as the thing said, "Let me show you."

It snapped its fingers, which were grotesquely long, and the world froze.

Everyone in the crowd stayed completely still as if they couldn't move. Mr. Getty had his hand raised, pointing to the marsh. He hadn't even finished what he was going to say. The men held torches, their mouths open as if yelling, but they issued forth no sound. Libby looked pleased, and Matthew clung to Zofia's spirit cabinet. Abigail too was frozen in place. She remained on the ground, kneeling near her father's feet, pulling at his pant leg, in a silent display of begging him to show mercy.

"I can give you power," the thing said. "You can get back at these small souls for the wrongs done to you."

Zofia wasn't sure what that meant.

"Trust me," the thing said. "All you have to do is let me in. Then all of this"—it waved its long arm to indicate the crowd, the torches, the improvised pyre, and Mr. Getty—"all of this will be of no consequence. You will have immortality as well as vengeance."

"No," she said, and her voice trembled. This was exactly what Mr. Getty wanted to think of her—that she was evil.

"So you want to be burned alive?" the thing questioned, its voice smooth as silk. Tempting.

"I'm not evil," Zofia said.

"Ah, but you will suffer the consequences, nevertheless. You shall be burned alive." It paused, regarded her. "Or, you could make a different choice."

Zofia quaked in her still-wet boots. She didn't know what to do. She didn't want to burn to death, and she didn't think she could make it across the bay to safety—especially not now. The water was higher than ever.

At that moment, an alligator swished out of the marsh and settled in near Zofia's feet. She recognized the beast—it was the one she'd saved from the debris in the center of town.

"This one is ready to let me in," the thing said.

The alligator growled as if in response and seemed to smile. The thing pulled a black, moving ball from the area around its chest, though its form remained unchanged. It brought the swirling ball close to the alligator and the ball spread out, like a vapor. It covered the alligator from snout to tail and then dissolved into the beast's skin, absorbed.

The change in the alligator was slight but did not escape Zofia's notice. The animal became unstable, more like the thing. Moving, jolting, vibrating.

It was an alligator, but also not an alligator any longer. It growled again and Zofia thought it sounded different—not happy but satisfied.

The thing snapped its long fingers and the crowd again yelled. They raised their weapons and thrust them toward Zofia. Mr. Getty finished his terrible sentence with "...get out, and never return."

The thing again snapped its fingers and silence settled on the world again. It turned to Zofia. "Are you willing to let me in, and be done with these puny folk or would you rather face their wrath?"

The alligator didn't look harmed. And after a few moments of tense, heart-wrenching trembling, Zofia was convinced: she had no other choice. It was death or try this...trust this thing. "I'll do it," she breathed.

The thing pulled another black, moving ball from its body and held it out in its long, long fingers toward Zofia.

The ball moved to hover around her. It melted into her.

Zofia knew the chill of the spiritual world. Many spirits had touched her and one or two had passed directly through her body, so she knew the cold that came from that realm. This, however, was unlike anything she had ever encountered. She was freezing.

But she felt something else too—a power rippling through her.

"Good," the thing said. "Let these souls know their place. Punish them."

It snapped its long fingers, and the world unfroze once more.

The crowd around her roared to life. Mr. Getty pointed to the marsh and yelled at her to go. The crowd jeered and threatened her with their torches. One man uncoiled a rope and said, "Bind her to the stake!" Another brought his torch close to the wood. "Burn the witch!" he yelled.

Zofia stood tall. She felt the gift the spirit had granted move through her. It was enticing and alluring, but an unmistakably evil power.

"Do it," the thing hissed into the night. "Destroy them."

The thing wanted her to kill everyone, to take the flames from their torches and turn them on the crowd, to move her hand in a way that would cut their throats or whip up a wind as strong as the storm and blow them to oblivion.

She fought against it.

"Burn the witch, burn the witch, burn the witch!"

No, she wouldn't kill. Instead, she drew on the power of the thing and stretched herself out until she towered over the crowd.

"There will be no burning here today. There will be no more death," she said. She waved her arm as if to indicate the ruined town. "Look around you. There is nothing but destruction as far as the eye can see. You will not take my life—for that life is already gone. I will go into the marsh." Here, Zofia moved closer to Mr. Getty. She bent down in his face. She let her coldness, her frigid breath, wash over him. "And you will let me be."

With that, she turned and walked into the marsh. The alligator followed. Together, they made their way to a small stand of trees.

Chapter Eighteen

Tourists were always in the Strand, swarming, shopping, lingering. But so were the locals. To be fair, it was a great place; there was something for everyone. There were shops for beach stuff and shops for perfumes. Shops for toys and for jewelry. There were restaurants and places to get a cold drink and a small grassy area with a plaque commemorating Juneteenth.

I could tell when we were close because the roads went from regular pavement to bumpy brick cobblestones, with trolley lines here and there. Nana skidded to a stop in a parking spot.

She climbed off the scooter and wiped her brow—not from sweat. More like she felt lucky to be alive.

I did too.

"Those cobblestones are tricky on two wheels," I said, guessing at what had her feeling anxious.

She nodded.

Gracie pulled over next to us and threw down the kickstand.

"Let's go," I said. "Down here, Nana?" I pointed, anxious to be on our way.

Gracie stared up at a sign about parking. "We have to pay," she said.

Nana patted her fanny pack and looked disappointed.

"Do you have your wallet in there or something?" I asked.

NURSING HOME WON'T GIVE IT TO ME WITHOUT "ADULT SUPERVISION."

"Whatever," I said with a wave of my hand. "It doesn't matter."

"We have to pay," Gracie said again.

"We don't have to do anything," I told her. "We're kids. They're scooters."

Nana pointed to herself, her right eyebrow raised.

"The scooters belong to a couple of kids," I amended. "What are they going to do—ticket us?"

"I think there's an app Mom uses," Gracie said, and she tugged out her phone.

"Gracie," I said, exasperation getting the better of me. It was hot and I was tired, and Gracie wasn't listening. "Mom uses her phone because she has her credit card information stored on it. We don't have a credit card."

Gracie still tapped on the phone screen. "Maybe I can download it and log in as Mom." She glanced up at the sign again.

"Gracie!" I yelled. "We have to break this rule, okay? We are not paying for parking! We need to GO!" I was huffing by then, anger taking over. I might have even been flailing my arms and stomping my feet.

A beat. Nana and Gracie stared at me, their mouths hanging open.

I came to my senses. "Sorry," I said. "I know, I know, I lost it. But we have to go. Think of Mom and Duck and Tofu."

Nana was the first to come over to my side. She made a sweeping motion with her arm, which I took to mean, *Yeah, forget paying for parking. Follow me.*

Great. We were on the same page again.

Gracie, sulking just a little, followed. So on we went.

By the time we were three blocks down, Nana was moving slowly.

"Are you okay?" I asked her.

She looked tired but she flexed her bicep, like she was ready to take on the world.

"Are we close?"

Nana pointed at a store several doors down. Super. We were just about there.

Bells on top of the door to Odds and Ends jingled at our entrance.

As we stepped inside, the AC blew down on us and it felt so good, I took a moment to enjoy it, imagining the pools of sweat evaporating from my body.

When I opened my eyes, I looked around. This place was incredible. I'd pictured some sleepy antique shop filled with creepy dolls and dusty silverware, but that wasn't the vibe. This shop had colorful display tables and interesting stuff. There were vintage postcards, hand-knitted cat toys, a bunch of soaps, and what looked like really old menorahs and little three-legged clay pigs.

"This is something else," I said to Nana.

She nodded, because it was.

Gracie agreed.

"Let's do it," I said, and I moved to the closest shelves, where there were old books and hand-painted greeting cards and framed photographs. I took my time in case there was anything about the witch, but nothing seemed relevant. It was all just old stuff. Gracie and Nana were riffling through a box of records, so I stepped farther into the store. I breezed by a collection of glasses so old they were frosted, and a bunch of ancient bottles that might have come off the *Titanic*. Not what I needed. Another step and I discovered an impressive collection of beaded necklaces and ceramic elephants.

Another step. A doctor's kit from forever ago. But nothing that looked like it belonged to the Alligator Witch.

When I got to the area near the cash register, an employee greeted me. She wore her hair in two braids, and a sweater that looked like it had been knitted by her favorite aunt.

"Hi," I said. "So this is going to sound odd, but I'm looking for something that has to do with the Alligator Witch."

"Oh, not odd at all," she said. "We get lots of tourists in here and they're all interested in the witch. Right this way." She came out from behind the register and led me to a table in the middle of the store. A bunch of things sat on it, but they were just souvenirs: alligator bumper stickers, alligator magnets, stuffed alligators wearing witch hats. They were ridiculous.

"This isn't exactly what I was hoping for," I said, and the employee, who'd started walking away, turned around.

"Oh?" she said.

I let out a breath, trying to figure out how to explain this. I finally came up with: "My grandfather came to this store in 1980 and bought something, something important to the Alligator Witch."

The girl's eyes went wide. "Hold on," she said. "My manager might know what you're talking about." She trotted off, leaving me wondering if this was real, if I was actually going to stumble on some kind of answer.

Gracie and Nana strolled over as I was waiting.

"Did you see anything?" I asked but their faces had already given me my answer: nothing but disappointment. Gracie shook her head. Nana frowned with the part of her face that worked but then brightened. She gestured at herself and a glass case nearby.

"Okay, thanks, Nana," I said as she moved off, ready to study the things inside.

When the store employee returned, she had an older man with her. He had kind eyes, and a graying mustache and beard. The girl deposited the man with me and Gracie, who was busy picking up every stuffed alligator and petting it, and walked away.

"Hi," I said to him. "I'm looking for things related to the Alligator Witch, but not stuff like this." I gestured to the touristy junk Gracie was admiring. "My grandfather came in here in 1980 and bought an accordion. It was just what he needed, just what he was looking for, because it belonged to the witch."

The manager's face turned grave, like he'd seen a ghost. "Yes," he said, "I remember. I was working that day."

A familiar voice cut through his tale: "Gracie! Lana!"

It was Nancy. Because *of course* Nancy was there right when I was about to get answers.

Nancy ran over to us, and in classic fashion, she was a whirlwind of polite hellos and it's-nice-to-see-yous and handshakes and pats on the back. "You met my uncle!" she said, and she sounded excited.

"Uncle?" I asked. She obviously meant the manager.

"Uncle Ben, these are my friends—Gracie and Lana."

"Oh," he said, tilting his head. "How interesting." He raised his eyebrows high at Nancy like he was asking a question without words.

She nodded in response to whatever her uncle wanted to know, her face as serious as I'd ever seen it, but then she dropped into her normal, happy demeanor. "I came by just to say hi," she said to him. "I've been shopping." She raised a bag from the most glorious candy store that ever existed: La King's Confectionary. She looked inside the bag and pulled out a flavored jelly candy in the shape of a fruit slice for each of us.

Then she turned to Gracie. "I have so much to tell you."

Gracie looked confused as she took this in. "I ... do ... too." Her words came out slowly.

"Really?" Nancy asked, peppy as ever. "What's up?"

"Uh, you first," Gracie said.

Nancy looped her arm through Gracie's and tugged her away, headed for the door.

I wanted with all my heart to stop this, to put on the brakes, to grab Gracie and hiss *Don't say a word!* in her ear. Or at least catch her eye and shake my head. But they were already gone, skipping through the shop, opening the door, and landing outside in the sunshine.

My hope was that whatever news Nancy had to share took so much time Gracie never got a chance to blurt out anything about our day. Or that Gracie would remember what I'd said this morning. Ugh. I'd have to make this fast.

I turned back to Nancy's uncle. "So, you remember the accordion?"

He tucked his hands in his pockets. "It was given to me under strictest orders to keep it safe. I didn't feel comfortable leaving it in my house. People"—here he let his eyes wander around the shop as if someone might be eavesdropping, and he lowered his voice—"people were looking for it."

His words were filled with ominous suggestions. "So you brought it here?"

A glint in his eyes looked like fear. "People were desperate to find it, but I hid it in the back room in a dusty old box."

"How did my papa get it?"

Nancy's uncle studied me for a long moment, like he was testing whether or not to trust me. "Your papa needed my help."

"So you just gave it to him?"

He pulled his hands from his pockets, rubbing them together, and let out a heavy breath through his nose. "I felt I could take his word for truth."

This was it! Great. All I had to do was convince him that I was trustworthy.

"I need your help too. I'm looking for something that used to belong to the witch. I promise my intensions are good. It's a matter of life and death."

He frowned. "I'm sorry; I have nothing."

"Nothing that you're willing to part with?"

He shook his head. "There's nothing to give."

"What do you mean?" I was getting frantic. "The witch said I needed to find what was hers."

The man rubbed his beard. "There is one other item that belonged to the witch... one last lost thing—"

"Where is it?" I couldn't help interrupting.

"I've been searching for it for years. Many people have." He shook his head again in that slow, sad way. "No one can find it."

"But—" I started.

Nancy's uncle took my hand in his. Kind of like a handshake, but one that was wishing me well, one that said he wouldn't be able to help me. "I wish I could tell you more. I'm sorry."

So that was it.

There was nothing here. Nothing to find. Even though Nancy's uncle was the closest thing I had to a lead, he was a dead end.

But it couldn't be over! "What about a guy named Matthew? I've heard if I can find him, I can find the witch's stuff."

He tilted his head, like he was considering every Matthew he knew.

"Maybe someone who works here, or who used to?" I asked.

"We don't have any employees by that name. Sorry." He turned and went into the back room, leaving me to my misery.

I plodded over to Nana, who was bent over, still inspecting the things in that glass case. "We should go," I said. Sadness filled my voice. "There's nothing here for us."

She looked confused. She went to unzip her fanny pack, but I put my hand over hers.

"It's not here," I said. "I'm sure. We have to go. We have to... figure out what to do next." My feet felt like they weighed twenty pounds each as we lumbered toward the door.

Out, back into the sunshine, back into the heat.

It felt worse now—pizza-oven worse.

I spotted Gracie and Nancy on a bench a few storefronts down from Odds and Ends. Gracie stood up as I approached them. "Don't be mad," she said.

I knew it. I knew it! I triple knew it! She'd told Nancy. She'd blabbed, spilled the beans, let the cat out of the bag. Dang it. Dang it, dang it, dang it.

"Don't be mad," she said again.

I didn't have the inner strength to even respond to her; I just rolled my eyes and pinched the bridge of my nose.

"Don't be mad," she repeated.

Too late for that. "Gracie," I said. "Why?" I held my arms out and let the exasperation I felt fill my voice. "Why? *Why?*"

"She can help," Gracie sputtered. "Nancy can help us."

"Sure, right, she can help. And I'm Spider-Man with awesome, amazing superpowers."

"No, really," Gracie insisted.

"Just tell me this. Did she already call the cops or is she about to?"

"No, no," Gracie said, like she was pleading with me. "You don't get it."

"Really," Nancy said, standing up and butting in, "I think I can help."

Her idea of *help* wasn't going to do us any good.

I turned my anger on her. "Did you call the fire department or an ambulance?"

"Neither, as of this moment," Nancy said.

Gracie said, "Lana, listen to her."

But my brain assured me *Nancy cannot help*. With a giant huff, I turned and started back toward the scooters. "Come on, Nana," I said.

"Lana!" Gracie grabbed my arm and spun me around. "She knows who Matthew is."

"What?" I was having trouble processing those words. "No way. She does not." If Nancy's uncle didn't know who Matthew was, there was no way Nancy knew. This was just Nancy being Nancy. Nancy trying to help. Nancy wasting our time.

Nancy said, "His full name was Matthew Getty, and at one point he had *all* the witch's things."

Nana, who was close behind me, made a noise that sounded half angry, half surprised. Like she'd heard what Nancy said, and she wasn't happy about it.

"Getty?" I let the name swirl in my brain. "Like the Getty Mansion?"

"Yup," Nancy said.

The Getty Mansion was a historic house on Broadway Avenue J. Every time we'd driven past it with Dad, he'd talked about how it was one of the oldest structures in Galveston.

Nancy beamed at me like she had this whole mystery solved. "Come on," she said. "We need to go see my mom. She'll know what to do."

Her mom? Was this for real?

Nancy spun on a dime and practically flew up the street, headed in the opposite direction, away from where we'd parked our scooters. "Follow me," she said over her shoulder, and she waved her hand like she expected us to run right behind her.

Gracie did. "Come on," she said over her shoulder to us. "I really think she can help."

I stood in the summer heat and considered the options. In short: there was only one. "She's either onto something," I mumbled to Nana, "or this is going to be a monumental waste of time. Not sure which."

Nana shrugged and gestured toward the girls.

"You're right," I said. "I guess we should go." Nana and I started down the sidewalk together, following Gracie and Nancy, headed toward the ocean.

Chapter Nineteen

The Strand petered out about a block from the water. At that point, other businesses took over—dolphin tours and seafood restaurants and historical museums.

I watched Nancy's back. She strutted like she had all the answers, and after a few minutes, I knew where we were going: the Galveston Historical Society. Her mom worked there.

Even though Nancy had said her mom could help, I knew it wasn't true. What could she do? But at least she was cool. She let Nancy do whatever she wanted. Whenever Gracie slept over, they had an amazing time; they'd go crabbing with leftover chicken. Or hit the Historic Pleasure Pier and ride the Iron Shark Roller Coaster. Or get ice cream at eleven o'clock at night.

Was I jealous? Maybe a little. Kaylee's and Julianna's moms didn't take us anywhere when we had sleepovers. Their moms, like mine, always said no.

A bunch of pelicans huddled on the sidewalk near the entrance of the historical society, looking at us patiently like we were there to see them. Like we had fish to hand over for their lunch.

"We don't have anything for you," Nancy said cheerily to them. "Sorry." They sidestepped as she approached, turning their adorable, round, dark eyes on me and Nana, like we were surely the ones with fish in our pockets.

"Sorry, guys," I said.

Nancy opened the front door and led us inside. The historical society was filled with displays—one about something old followed by another about something even older. There was information about the railroad. Stuff on immigrants. Old telephones you could pick up and listen to someone talk about the job they worked a long time ago. In the far corner, there were chairs set up and a documentary playing on a small screen. Even from where I stood, I could tell it was about the Big Storm—the hurricane that hit the island in 1900.

Dad knew all about the storm, and because of that, so did I. I knew that there was a wall of water sixteen feet high that hit the shore on the night of September eighth and wiped out most of the buildings in Galveston. I knew that nearly 8,000 people had died. And I knew that they raised the entire island eight feet after that and built the seawall that covered over ten miles of shoreline.

Nancy's mom sat at a small desk just inside the door—the only employee—and we were the only ones inside.

Nancy said, "Good thing it's a slow day. Mom, we need a special showing." She pointed at the documentary.

What now?

Nancy's mom took us all in. She cocked her head at Nana like she was baffled by her presence. "You're sure?" she said to Nancy, who answered, "Yes."

Nancy rounded the desk to stand near her mom. In a hushed voice, she said, "You remember that hypothetical situation we discussed—the one about the Alligator witch?"

Her mom nodded.

"Well . . . ," Nancy said, and she jutted her chin at me.

Nancy's mom looked shocked. Then she looked amazed. Then she turned to blink at me with alarm in her eyes. "Really?" she asked.

I didn't answer because I wasn't sure if she was talking to me or Nancy. But I knew one thing for sure: this was code. Code for

I had been the one who'd bothered the witch. Code for *I had been the one who'd messed up.* Well, I had. I was glad Nancy and her mom used this code since I didn't want Nana to know. Not yet.

When Nancy's mom turned back to Nancy, she looked grim. "Well then," she said, "we certainly do need a special showing."

She came out from behind the desk and held out her hand to Nana. "Hello, Mrs. Parker. It's nice to see you again." There was something in her voice—a strained quality. Like she hated Nana but was trying to hide it, to be polite in front of us kids.

Nana sucked in a breath as if she'd just realized who this lady was. Her right hand rose to her chest, and one of her eyebrows furrowed. It looked to me like she hated Nancy's mom too. I had no idea what was going on.

Nancy's mom kept her hand out until Nana took it...grudgingly. "I'm glad to see you're up and about," she said.

Nana nodded. These two clearly had a history. I scanned my memories, trying to figure out when, where, or how they might have met. Nancy's mom had been to our house plenty of times, mostly to pick up Gracie or to drop off Nancy. But I couldn't remember when she might have met Nana. This beef between them was baffling.

Gracie was studying a sign at the front desk. It listed the suggested donation for admission to the exhibits. "Do we need to pay?" she asked, sounding worried again.

"Gracie, get off it," I snapped.

"What?" she asked.

Clueless.

I rolled my eyes because *really?*

"What?" she asked again.

"Just forget it."

Nancy's mom turned to us and brightened. "You don't need to pay, not today. Not for this."

"Alligator showings are special cases," Nancy said.

Alligator showings. What could that mean?

"I'll start it from the beginning," Nancy's mom said. She took out an iPad from a drawer in the desk, then she strode toward the documentary area. Nancy ushered us to the chairs set up near the screen.

When we were settled, Nancy's mom pressed a few buttons on her iPad and the film started rolling.

It was boring. It was made up of pictures of historic Galveston, with narration by a male voice droning on about what the city was like back in 1900. I mean, Dad would have loved it, but it was a snooze-fest for anyone who didn't have a PhD in history.

Then it stopped.

"Hold on while Mom enlarges it," Nancy said. She crossed her arms and leaned closer to the screen as if she was anticipating something to happen, something more than an unimpressive account of a storm that happened forever ago.

The narrator had been talking about the Galveston boardwalk around the turn of the twentieth century. A woman in the foreground wore a long white dress that went up to her neck and down to her ankles. Worst outfit for a summer day, ever. She held a parasol. Behind her were people strolling the boardwalk and the shops and hotels. It looked like any old day A Long Time Ago.

Nancy's mom did something to zoom in on the area behind the woman's shoulder in the photograph. We could see a crowd gathered around another woman who held out her arms. When Nancy's mom enlarged the image again, something about the woman looked familiar.

"Is that...?" I started. Her hair was in a bun. Her dress was long and dark. Her face was in profile, but it kind of looked like... and then I saw what was in the air around her. Objects.

An accordion. A tambourine. A candelabra.

Holy crumbs!

"It's the witch!" I spouted.

"Her name was Zofia Kowalczyk. Hard to say. Harder to spell," Nancy said.

"The witch was a real person?" Gracie said, sounding surprised.

"She was," Nancy answered. "No one knows where she was born, but she lived in New York City, and she came to Galveston in 1900."

"How on earth do you know that?" I blurted.

"Reading, research, and family history," Nancy said. She said this like it made sense.

Nancy's mom walked toward the screen and nodded at it. "Look at the item on the ground near her feet, Lana. That's the last item, the one thing still missing."

"In other words," Nancy said, "that's what you're looking for."

Could this day get any wilder?

I stood and went to the screen. What was it? A rectangular... something, sitting on the boardwalk, a few feet away from the witch. About three feet high. It maybe had doors. "What is it?"

"That's Zofia's spirit cabinet. Her most prized possession," Nancy's mom said.

Nancy said, "It's been missing for a long time."

I remembered what Nancy's uncle had said to me in the store—that there was one thing left, that he had been looking for it. "If it's been missing for a long time, how am *I* going to find it?"

"You're going to find it," Nancy said with what looked like a wink, "because you have a clue. A clue that no one has ever had before."

"A clue?" Nancy's mom raised her eyebrows and walked toward our row of chairs. "Tell me everything. Be specific."

Nancy took over before I could get a word out. "The witch said that if they found *Matthew*, they could find the spirit cabinet. It has to be Matthew Getty, right?"

Nancy's mom's mouth fell open. "Matthew Getty," she said quietly, and she repeated, "Matthew Getty. Find him and you find the lost object." She was mumbling now, almost to herself, like she was considering this, taking in Nancy's interpretation and seeing if it worked. "It has to be," she agreed.

"Well, let's go find him," I said. "If you know where he lives, just tell me. I'll be there before you can say, *Dang, that Lana is fast*."

"That's the thing," Nancy said. She and her mom shared a look before she continued, "He's dead."

Chapter Twenty

"Dead?" I asked. My heart sank.

"He died a long time ago," Nancy's mom answered. "He was a young man when Zofia lived in Galveston."

Zofia... the girl in the picture, the witch. "Did they know each other?" I asked.

Nancy nodded. "They were not friends. Emphasis on the *not*."

"He took her things," Nancy's mother said, "right after the Big Storm. His father believed Zofia had used evil magic to bring the hurricane; Matthew assumed her possessions had magical powers, so he stole them from her. He swore he'd never give them back."

"Oh," I said. My mind was moving slowly, like a muddy river. I looked over at Nana, who sat up in the chair like she was at attention. Half of her face was concentrated, focused.

"What do you think?" Nancy's mom asked Nana.

Why was she asking Nana?

Nana pulled out her notepad and wrote, WHAT THEY'RE SAYING IS TRUE.

"About Matthew Getty?" Gracie asked.

She nodded. Now Nana seemed to know stuff too? This day was moving past *weird* and barreling toward *clearly bizarre*.

I paced. It was the only way I could think. Nancy, her mom, and Nana believed there was something to this Matthew Getty thing. They thought I had to find him. But how was I supposed to do that?

"He's dead. Okay." Was I talking out loud to myself? Yeah, we'd reached that point. "He's dead and gone but he might still have the spirit cabinet with him, if he really cared about keeping it away from the witch. She was a medium, so she could talk to the dead... Maybe that's how she knows he still has it. Maybe she... spoke to him. Maybe he told her he still had it."

"I think you're right, Lana," Nancy said.

"Great," I said. "All we have to do is get to him."

Nancy and her mom shared another look before Nancy said, "I think I know where we need to go."

⸺⸺⸺

After hanging a **SORRY, WE'RE CLOSED** sign on the front door, Nancy's mom led us to a parking lot around back. "I don't think this is a good idea," she said. It was mostly directed at Nancy.

Nancy begged, "Please, Mom. We have to try. It's the obvious starting place."

Her mom sighed.

Nancy made her eyes look uber sad and turned her mouth down into an exaggerated frown. "Please, please? For me? I promise we'll be careful."

Her mom was hesitating, thinking it over. "And respectful?" she asked.

"Of course we'll be respectful," Nancy said. "Of course." As she said this, she raised three fingers like she was taking a Girl Scouts pledge or something equally dorky. "You have to let us try," Nancy pleaded. "If it doesn't seem possible, we'll find another way."

Nancy's mom moved her shoulders in a way that suggested she was giving up. She said, "If you promise to be respectful."

"Thanks, Mom," Nancy said. "It'll be fine, you'll see."

Nancy's mom's car was a big old clunker covered with bumper

stickers that announced all sorts of things—from **SUPPORT THE GIRL SCOUTS** to **COEXIST** to **HUMANKIND—BE BOTH**.

Nancy, Gracie, and I squished into the back seat. Nana took the front.

"So, where are we going?" I asked, bunching up my legs so I would fit. I got the middle. Lucky me.

"Evergreen Cemetery," Nancy announced, "where the entire Getty family is buried."

"You've got to be kidding me," Gracie said. She didn't sound thrilled with the prospect of visiting a cemetery.

I swallowed. Not what I expected either. "We have to try... everything," I pointed out.

"Exactly," Nancy said.

The cemetery was in the heart of the city, on Broadway Avenue J, not far from the historical society, but we caught so many red lights that the ride seemed to stretch out, making it feel like we'd traveled all the way off the island and back again.

Nancy jumped out of the car when we arrived and scurried toward the front gate. Everyone else moved slower.

Cemeteries had a thing about them. A silence. An unease. A spookiness, even in the middle of the day. The walkways of this one were well-maintained, and the grass was somehow green, despite the sweltering sun, but I still shivered.

"Come on," Nancy urged. She waved us forward.

Mom had had Dad's body cremated and she had spread his ashes in the ocean the fall after he passed. Looking at these graves with people's names on them and flowers or ribbons or little tokens made me wish we'd done things differently. I wanted a place like this to visit, a solid location where I could feel close to Dad, where I could leave him something or go talk to him. I had nothing like that. Not even an urn to hold. It made me feel empty. I glanced at Gracie and saw tears shining in her eyes.

Crumbs.

To Nancy, it seemed like a cemetery was just a cemetery. Not a scary place, not a sad place. Just where we needed to go to get the job done. She headed farther in. *Might as well catch up*, I thought. Stay focused. I called, "Hey, hold up," and went after her.

Gracie was right behind me as we rushed toward the older part of the cemetery. There were grand mausoleums back there. The people buried in this part had money and lots of it, and they wanted everyone to know. Even in death.

Nancy pointed toward the way back. "The Getty plot is over there."

I wanted to ask her how she knew that, but I wasn't sure I wanted to know the answer, so I kept my mouth shut.

We finally arrived at the biggest, fanciest mausoleum. It was like a whole house—four walls, a roof, pretty stonework on the corners. It towered over the others nearby, as if it was judging them for being less than. The thing had to be as big as our living room and kitchen combined. Why would you need so much space after you died?

There was a plaque on the facade.

PERCIVAL GETTY 1858-1924
MATTHEW GETTY 1884-1962
WILLIAM GETTY 1919-1979
ELOISE GETTY 1954-

Matthew! Seeing the name pushed every morose thought from my mind. Sure, I still missed Dad and wished I had a grave to visit, and sure, I still thought cemeteries were creepy, but my sense of mission took over. Today was about rescuing Mom and Duck and Tofu—if I could get to Matthew Getty, I could do that.

A sudden thought hit: that spirit cabinet could be in there, with his coffin. He could have even specified that in his will—*Put it in there right next to me.*

"Please," I said quietly. I wasn't sure who or what I was pleading with. Maybe the witch. Maybe the ghost of Matthew Getty. Maybe just my lucky stars. "Please..."

"We've got to get in and look around...," Nancy said, "but respectfully."

"In?" Gracie asked. She sounded as not-thrilled about this as I felt.

"Well, yeah," Nancy said. "If Matthew has it, it's going to be in there."

I gulped.

Did I really want to go *inside* a mausoleum? Heck no! It was filled with dead people. Not just Matthew, but his father and son, from the looks of things. Plus, the other beings that might be in there—spiders and snakes and other creepy, crawly reptiles. I wasn't a fan of that kind of nature.

There seemed to be no other way, though. I shuddered, clamped my lips together, and moved toward the door to the mausoleum. "Let's get this over with."

I shoved my hand against the metal door. It made a creaking sound, like it was acknowledging my show of strength, but it didn't move. I shoved harder. Nothing. "Come on!" I blurted.

"Uh, Lana," Nancy said, "I don't think you're going to be able to open it like that."

"Yeah," Gracie said. "Looks pretty solid from here."

"So what do we do?" I shot back.

"First, we look for windows," Nancy declared. She circled the structure and returned a moment later, looking less chipper. I didn't have to ask what she'd found.

"Is there a crack we can look through?" Gracie asked.

Nana and Nancy's mom reached the mausoleum. Nana was clutching Nancy's mom's arm like somewhere along the way she'd needed support. My heart filled with shame. I should have been there for her. Heck, she didn't even like Nancy's mom. I'd hurried off without her, and now she looked worn out. Crumbs.

"How're you doing, Nana?" I asked, walking up to meet them. She nodded like she was okay, but I could see the truth.

I pointed to the mausoleum. "We're trying to find a way inside."

"But we're doing it respectfully!" Nancy added.

"I don't think this will work, girls," Nancy's mom said.

"Yeah, but... we need to try," Nancy insisted.

Gracie was inspecting the door now, touching it like a hidden passage would suddenly spring open. Hint: one didn't. "There's a keyhole, but I can't see in," she said. "Does anyone have a flashlight?"

A keyhole...

"Hold on!" I nearly yelled. "I have a key!" I tugged Dad's key from around my neck. "Maybe this opens it." I ran up to the door, pushing Gracie out of the way, and shoved the key in. It wiggled and jiggled. The hole was too big. Cavernous. Like it was made for a real, honest-to-goodness skeleton key, not the small one I held.

"Dang it," I said. I pulled the key out, backed up a few steps, and hung it around my neck again.

"Why did you think Dad's key would open Matthew Getty's gravesite?" Gracie asked. She said it without hostility, but it felt like a kick in the stomach.

"I don't know," I said with a moan. "It's a key and it has something to do with the Alligator Witch, and I guess"—here I stamped my foot on the grass—"you just never know."

Nancy patted my shoulder in a consoling way.

Ugh.

"What do we do now?" I asked, and I kicked at a clump of grass. "Head back to the car?" Sweat was gathering on my forehead and upper lip.

Nana had been busy scratching out a note, and now she held out her pad. *LANA, YOU HAVE YOUR DAD'S KEY?*

"Yeah," I admitted. "I found it at your old house. Sorry, I should have asked before taking it, but I didn't know what it unlocked and I really wanted to know. I'd heard the witch could communicate with the dead, so I went into the marsh to find her. That's why she froze Mom and Duck and Tofu."

Nana's face became a thundercloud. *YOU BOTHERED THE WITCH?* she wrote. Under it, in even bigger letters, she wrote, *YOU WENT INTO THE MARSH?*

Crumbs again. I'd known truth time was coming, but I still wasn't ready. "I'm sorry, Nana. You always told me not to go into the marsh and you always told me to leave that witch alone. I should have listened. I really, really should have." Tears stung my eyes. "I didn't think she was real, or I didn't know for sure, or I just wanted to try, anyway. But I get it now. She's mean, just like you said. I'm so sorry."

Half of Nana's face was the picture of disappointment.

"I'm trying to fix it," I said. "I'm doing my best." It sounded like my throat was filled with scratchy wool.

Nana nodded, then let go of her half frown. *YOUR PAPA BOTHERED HER ONCE TOO. PEOPLE MAKE MISTAKES*, she wrote.

"Papa did?" I asked.

THAT'S WHY I GOT FROZEN AND WHY HE WENT LOOKING FOR THE ACCORDION.

Duh. I had never considered how it happened, but of course he'd gone into the marsh. I wiped my hand across my nose, which was running. "I'm sorry," I said again, and let out a slobbery sob, which was embarrassing.

Gracie said gently, "It's okay, Lana. We'll figure it out."

"But how?" My voice was weak. The storm inside me was dissipating; a rain shower of sadness was taking the place of the hurricane of despair. Boy, it was weird to have *Gracie* be the one comforting *me*.

"I have another idea!" Nancy shouted. She stood near the plaque, the one with the Gettys' names on it. "*Someone* in the Getty family is still alive." She pointed to the bottom name. Eloise. It had a birth date, but not a death date.

"You want to go see Eloise Getty?" Nancy's mom said, sounding unhappy.

"I think we have to," Nancy said with a shrug. "She must have the key."

Nana made some grunting noises like she was upset about this idea too, and Nancy's mom patted her on the arm. "I know, Mrs. Parker. I don't like it either. I suppose Nancy's right, though. Eloise is probably the only one who can help us."

At that, Nana grunted again.

"What do you know about Eloise Getty?" I asked Nana.

This day... could it get any stranger?

She wrote, *ELOISE GETTY IS NOT A NICE WOMAN.*

"Does she live in town?" I asked.

"She does," Nancy said. "In the Getty Mansion, of course."

Well then, our next stop was decided.

I made sure to walk back through the cemetery with Nana. She draped an arm over my shoulder, and I put one of mine around her waist. We had just about reached the car when she stopped to write something on her notepad. She flashed it to me. *YOUR DAD'S KEY OPENS PAPA'S TRUNK. THE ONE IN THE STORAGE UNIT. THE ONE WE FOUND THE JOURNAL IN TODAY.*

I was about to ask her how she knew that, not to mention how she got that trunk open since she hadn't asked me for the key, when she unzipped her fanny pack and pulled out a golden key on a thin blue ribbon. The ribbon was the same color as the one around my neck, but much, much smaller, like someone had cut a tiny piece from my ribbon and tied it onto hers. I sucked in a breath and unwound Dad's key from my neck. I held the key out and Nana placed hers on top of it. Exactly the same—the same ridges and teeth and cuts and grooves.

"What the...?" I wasn't even sure what question I wanted to ask.

She tucked her key away and wrote, *I'LL TELL YOU ABOUT IT IN THE CAR.*

We climbed back in, and—thank all that's good in the world—Nancy's mom cranked the AC. Nana started writing immediately, and at the third red light, she reached back and handed me her notepad. The handwriting was neat and careful; she'd taken her time with this note.

Papa died when your dad was fifteen, and it broke his heart. It was a hard time. Sometimes he felt like he couldn't make it through the day. He missed his father so much. I had gathered Papa's things and put them in the trunk, which I shut tight and shoved into the spare room. I didn't know your dad cared one way or another about Papa's things until one day I found him huddled in the spare room with the trunk open and all of Papa's belongings around him, spread out on the rug. I didn't like to see Papa's treasured items because they reminded me of what I'd lost, but they did the opposite for your dad. They made him feel close to his father, helped him remember. That day, we moved the trunk into his room. He kept the key to the trunk around his neck, maybe as a reminder of Papa—that he was never far from him. The day your dad went off to college, he gave me a copy of the key that he'd had made. He said he didn't want Papa to be far from me either. Your dad—he wore that key even after he married your mother and had you girls. I think he wanted his father to be a part of his life, and that was how he did it. I keep the key he gave me now—still—in memory of your dad, and his Papa.

"Wow," I said. "I had no idea."

Nana, who'd been watching me from the front seat, nodded.

Gracie's phone pinged. She was texting someone. Because of course she was. "Hey, don't tell whoever you're texting about what's going on," I said.

Nancy's phone pinged next. She was furiously tapping on the screen.

Gracie gave me a look like I was dumb. "She already knows what's going on." She jutted her chin toward Nancy.

My head swiveled to look at Nancy, who'd just hit Send on a message. Gracie's phone pinged again.

"You're texting each other?" I asked. "You know you're sitting in the same car, right? You're like two feet from each other." Aggravation crept into my voice.

"You're in between us," Gracie said.

Was she serious? *Come on.*

"Whatever you're saying to each other you can say in front of me," I snapped. "Don't tell secrets like I'm not good enough to hear them."

"No secrets," Gracie said, sulking. "We're just chatting."

"Well then, do it out loud."

"Girls." Nancy's mom cleared her throat. "We're here."

I looked out the window and saw we were in the long driveway of the Getty Mansion.

Chapter Twenty-One

And so the story of Zofia Kowalczyk comes nearly to a close. And yet, there is one more part I must tell, from my own point of view.

The townspeople cheered as Zofia moved into the marsh, like a prisoner going to their death. The men, with their torches and their weapons, felt they had won. And while that should have brought calm, the sensation of violence kept rising. It prickled my skin, giving me goosebumps. The town had awakened something deadly, something ready and longing for a sacrifice.

As I watched my friend disappear into the gloaming, I felt a crushing sense of despair.

The world had darkened. Not just physically.

Violence was here to stay.

It would be no use begging my father for mercy, this much I knew. He had prevailed and I had not.

I turned, hoping to start home in search of quiet, when my sister's voice stopped me.

"I will make sure that witch never leaves the marsh. It is my duty from here on out. I take that as my oath," Libby declared to the crowd.

Father nodded approvingly at her.

My brother, Matthew, spoke up next. "I vow to keep Galveston safe from the witch's things. No one will ever use them for evil again." He clutched Zofia's spirit cabinet to his chest.

I knew my siblings; their minds were set, their hearts were hardened. The only thing I could do was to make my own oath.

Right there, in the cooling night by the marsh, I whispered: "I will keep history safe. I will remain faithful to Zofia Kowalczyk, who I know was not a witch. I will prove this, someday. This is my vow."

I thank you, gentle reader, for hearing my tale. My greatest hope is that one day the truth will come out!

—*Abigail Getty*

Chapter Twenty-Two

I'd seen the Getty Mansion countless times, but it looked different today. Imposing and solid. Ageless.

"How old is this place?" I asked after climbing out of the car.

Gracie stood with her arms crossed and said softly, "Dad would have known."

"He would have," I agreed.

She gazed at the house. "I wish he was here."

"I do too," I said.

Nana still hadn't gotten out of the car. Through the window, I could see that her hands were gripping her thighs. I gave a small knock.

"It's time," I mouthed. I knew she knew this, but then why wasn't she out yet? Nancy and her mom were still in the car too.

In response, Nana shook her head.

I knocked again, lightly. "Nana."

She stayed put.

I gave the window a louder *thunk*.

Still, she sat.

This was Nana for you. As stubborn as a cat who'd found a patch of sunshine and wasn't going to budge.

"Nana," I said through the glass, trying to keep my voice calm while also loud enough to make sure she could hear, "we need you."

Finally, she cracked open the door and came out.

"What was that about?" I asked.

She turned to that page in her notepad from earlier—the one about how Eloise Getty wasn't a nice person—and flashed it my way.

"You really don't like her, huh?" I asked.

She seemed to think about it for a moment before giving a short, quick shake of her head.

"Well, how does she feel about you?" Mom always said that relationships went two ways.

Nana shook her head again, but slower.

"Great," Gracie said with a groan. "How are we going to get this mean woman who already doesn't like our family to talk to us?"

"We have to try." I said this because it was true. There was no other way. Ms. Getty almost certainly had the key to the Getty mausoleum—or access to it—and we needed to get her to help us. "Maybe you two can work out whatever went wrong in the past." She seemed to have done that pretty quickly with Nancy's mom.

Nana huffed out a breath like *fat chance*.

"Well, we're going in," I said.

Gracie tapped on the back seat window, motioning for Nancy to roll it down. "You guys aren't coming?"

Nancy opened the window and said, "If you want any chance of convincing Eloise to give you that key, we should stay here. It's a long story."

"Does this lady have a problem with *everyone* in town?" I asked.

Nana wrote, LOTS OF HISTORY.

Gracie said to me, "Maybe we should go in alone—just you and me?" She sounded terrified, but she added, "If Nana and Ms. Getty hate each other, maybe it would be better that way."

Nana wrote, SHE DOESN'T HATE ME, and then, I CAN BE

NICE. And with that, she seemed to stand taller. She took my arm and breathed in a deep breath.

"Let's get that key," I said.

―⋅―

The woman who answered the door was old, and as she stood in the doorway, she looked like a sentinel. One with makeup and a fancy dress.

"Hello," she said, and her eyes moved from me to Gracie, and then stopped on Nana, like they'd gotten stuck there. "Mrs. Parker," she said after a moment. There was surprise in her voice—and a trace of venom. She added, "How nice to see you."

Hint: she didn't think it was nice at all.

"Hello, Ms. Getty," I said, and the woman finally pried her eyes off Nana. "I hope you don't mind us dropping by. We would have contacted you first, but we didn't know we'd need your help until today, and it's urgent."

"You need my help?" she echoed, and a smile crept onto her face. It was a smile that made it seem like she had a secret she was keeping. "How... interesting."

"May we come in?" I didn't think we should discuss the key to a mausoleum standing on her doorstep. That, and it was hot.

"Please." She stepped aside to let us enter.

"I'm Lana Parker," I said, once we were all inside the front hall, "and this is my sister, Gracie. You already know my nana, it seems."

"Hello, girls."

There was a runner rug in the hallway and as Nana took a step, she tripped on it. It was her left leg that was giving her trouble. It had been dragging since Evergreen Cemetery.

"You okay, Nana?" I asked.

She caught her balance and nodded.

Ms. Getty laid a hand on her chest and said, "You poor thing, you've had quite a health scare." I guess she knew about Nana's stroke.

Nana attempted a brave smile with half of her face. It was clear she didn't want to talk about it.

"Well, I'm glad to see you're recovering," Ms. Getty said.

Nana took her notepad and wrote, GETTING STRONGER EACH DAY, THANK YOU.

"Oh my," Ms. Getty said, her hand still on her chest, "it took away your ability to speak. You poor, poor thing."

"She's doing great," I cut in. "She's been lifting weights and going to physical therapy and she'll be talking again before you know it."

"We won't be able to shut her up," Gracie added.

"Oh yes, I'm sure," Ms. Getty said dismissively. "Well, shall we take a seat in the dining room so you can impart the reason you've come by?"

"Yes," Gracie said. Then put in a quick, "Thank you, ma'am."

"Good, good." Ms. Getty shut the front door and waved a hand. "This way."

As she led us down the hall and through a grand foyer, I took a look around. This mansion was something else! High ceilings. A huge staircase. And the furniture—the furniture I could see from here—was big and sturdy and seemed like it could have survived five hurricanes. We stepped farther in, following Ms. Getty, and I caught sight of vast rooms to our right and our left. Oil paintings decorated the walls. Chandeliers hung down, sparkling in the afternoon light. This house was worth more money than I'd make in my lifetime.

"Here we are," Ms. Getty said as she led us through a doorway into a room with a long, elegant table that could seat at least a dozen people. She gestured at some chairs, like we should sit, and we did. All three of us, in a row.

She stayed standing. "I'll get us some refreshments," she said, and to Nana, she added, "You look worn out."

Ms. Getty tapped a screen built into the wall, some kind of digital intercom system, and said, "Patrick, Beatrice, to the formal dining room, please. Service for four." With another look at Nana, she added, "And plenty of ice water." When she released the button, she said to us, "It'll only be a moment. The help is quite good if one is willing to pay enough."

Half of Nana's face twitched, like she wanted to roll her eyes.

I got it. I did too. But I kept my features held in a polite mask.

Ms. Getty took a seat at the head of the table. "So you are here for my help. Perhaps you need money? A loan of some kind, Clementine?"

Nana crinkled up half of her lips like she wasn't pleased with Ms. Getty calling her by her first name and she slammed her notepad on the table, raising her pen to it as if to write, *No, that's not why we are here at all*, or something worse.

"Oh, this isn't about money," I said hastily.

"Oh?" Ms. Getty raised her eyebrows high.

"No, ma'am. It's about a key."

Before I could continue, a man in a dark blue suit entered the room.

"Oh, Patrick," she said, "there you are. These are my guests. They've dropped by for . . . well, I'm not sure what for, but let's offer them our finest refreshments, just as we'd serve family." She looked like she wanted to wink at Nana.

Patrick acknowledged us with the smallest folding of his mouth and bent to whisper something in Ms. Getty's ear.

I took the opportunity to lean in close to Nana. "How are you doing?" I said in a soft voice.

She just patted my hand.

"You've got this," I said. I didn't know if I meant that she could keep being nice to Ms. Getty or that she could make it through the rest of the day. Both, I hoped.

A sharp pang of guilt gripped me. I'd kept Nana away from her nursing home for hours. I'd made her walk all over town, ride a *scooter*, and traipse through a graveyard, and now I was forcing her to face a lady she obviously hated.

I said, "Sorry today's been hard on you."

Nana waved her hand like it was nothing.

Patrick disappeared through a doorway on the right, and Ms. Getty announced that muffins would arrive momentarily. "I had them made this morning," she said. "They're quite good. Healthful." She directed the last word at Nana as if Nana hadn't been taking care of herself adequately.

Truth be told: Ms. Getty was getting on my nerves, but I was looking forward to those muffins. I was starving. I had missed lunch, and it was 4:30.

A woman who also wore dark blue, but a dress instead of a suit, came in through the door Patrick had used. Probably Beatrice. She carried a tray holding a pitcher of water and four glasses. She poured the water. "Thank you," I said in a whisper. This house made you want to whisper. It was like a museum, and it had something about it—a feeling that you'd better behave, or you might get in trouble.

Nana drank down her whole glass in about two seconds flat.

"Oh my," Ms. Getty said. "Someone was thirsty."

"It's been quite a day," I said.

"Oh?"

"Quite a day," I repeated as Beatrice refilled Nana's glass. I paused. How did you ask someone for a key to open their family's mausoleum? I decided to back up a bit, go at the problem from a different angle. "I made a mistake this morning. I went to see the Alligator Witch."

"Nasty creature." Ms. Getty wrinkled up her face and looked like she might have said more, but Patrick returned with a tray full of muffins, four small plates, forks, knives, and napkins.

Oh good.

I could barely wait. My mouth watered. I was beyond hungry. As soon as he had the food in front of me, I went for that muffin like it was manna from heaven.

Total mistake. *Healthful*, in this place, obviously meant disgusting. It tasted like the worst cereal in the world with gross, hard nuts in the mix.

Gracie grabbed her muffin and took a huge bite too before looking really unhappy that she'd done that. She put it back on her plate.

Nana must have been *really* hungry because she scarfed down the whole thing.

"Bran muffins with walnuts," Ms. Getty said. She looked perfectly happy with the snack, although she hadn't touched hers. It sat in front of her while she ogled us.

I took another bite because first off, maybe my taste buds had been wrong and, well, I was hungry enough to do it, and secondly, because I didn't want to seem rude. But as I squished that nastiness around in my mouth, I had to try hard not to let on that it was the worst thing I'd ever tasted. I chewed and chewed and finally swallowed. That was it for me—starving or not. Yuck.

"So," Ms. Getty said, "you went to see the Alligator Witch, and it didn't work out so well."

"It didn't," I admitted. "She froze my mom and little sister with her magic." Saying it out loud to a stranger made it feel even more frightening. I shivered.

Ms. Getty didn't look surprised or frightened. She studied me for a moment. "Not a third? I've heard that witch takes three souls."

"She froze our cat too," I explained.

She *tsk*ed like I was a naughty child. "Cat?" she said. "I never heard of the witch freezing a cat. Or any other animal."

Ignoring her comment, I continued, "I never should have gone, and I regret it, but that's what happened."

"I'm sorry to hear it," she said.

"Thanks. The good news is that you can help," I said. "I just need to get an item that used to belong to the witch, and I think I know where it is. I know this sounds bizarre, but I was hoping that I could borrow the key to your family's mausoleum."

Now Ms. Getty looked surprised. She stopped all movement and stared at me for three long, sharp heartbeats.

"The one in Evergreen Cemetery," I clarified, in case she needed help remembering.

Still, she stared.

"Please?" I said as my heart hammered in my chest. She had to give it to me, she had to! "I have reason to believe the thing I need is in there."

She kept staring at me, without a word, as the room fell silent.

And then she let out a laugh. A real guffaw, like this all was hilarious. Her mouth opened wide, and she tilted her head back, laughing and laughing. Total enjoyment. I wondered if I'd missed something. Then, I wondered if she was just being mean. I glanced at Gracie, who blinked in obvious distress.

As Ms. Getty's laughter quieted and she seemed to gather her thoughts, she fixed her eyes on me. "Young lady, what do you think is in there that could possibly help you? My ancestors' decaying remains?"

I paused, unsure if I should tell her or not. It seemed best to be truthful. "The witch's spirit cabinet. It's made of wood and about three feet tall and—"

Ms. Getty cut me off. "Oh, my dear child, don't be foolish."

"I'm not," I said. "I got a clue this morning that pointed me to your family's mausoleum. The only problem is that it's locked."

"That is *not* the problem, believe me," she said. "The much bigger problem is that you don't know what you're talking about."

"Please!" I begged. "I do. I promise. And this is important. It's my family we're talking about. They're frozen! I *need* to borrow your key. I can have it back to you in an hour." It might have been a stretch, but I'd try to return it to her that quickly if she needed me to.

Gracie had her phone out; she was texting someone. Ugh. *Gracie*, I thought, *this is so not the time*, but I didn't say anything. In truth, I was hoping Ms. Getty wouldn't notice because she didn't seem like the type of person who would be pleased with a guest being on their phone in her presence.

Ms. Getty said, "Your information is dead wrong."

Dead wrong. The phrase struck me as particularly spiteful.

I took a deep breath and reached down in my gut until I found a way to respond in a manner that, if not quite reasonable, was at least not rude. "What do you mean, wrong? The spirit cabinet isn't there?"

"It's safe," she said with a glint in her eye.

"And you know where it is?" Another glint and a nod. I figured out right around then that I needed to treat this lady like a predator. My eyes darted to Gracie. I hoped to share a glance with her—see what she was thinking—but she was on her phone still. Ugh.

I stretched my hands, which had balled into fists. "I'm happy to hear you know all about the spirit cabinet," I said to Ms. Getty. "You seem to know a lot about Galveston's history. I've obviously come to the right place." A little flattery couldn't hurt.

"Oh, yes," she said, "you have."

I rearranged the fork and knife in front of me, stalling, trying to figure out what to say next to convince her to give me a hand. Gracie was texting away. Useless. I'd need to try a different tactic. "Can I pay you for the spirit cabinet?"

"I don't need your money," she answered, and gestured around the spacious room as if to say *I have everything I need and more*.

I thought, *Well, that's great for you, lady*, but didn't say it. I didn't say anything—too scared I'd blurt out something unkind.

Ms. Getty went on, "That item you mentioned—the spirit cabinet—was very important to my grandfather. He insisted that it stay in our family, close to him, always."

"Matthew Getty?" I asked. My breath hitched.

"Of course."

Gracie let out a noise like a gasp, and I looked over at her, glad she was paying attention at last. Only she hadn't heard the mention of Matthew Getty; she hadn't even looked up from her dang screen.

Ms. Getty continued, "I know he's watching over it still."

"But he's dead."

"Yes," she said, "but his spirit lives on."

"His spirit?" This made me think of the Alligator Witch and how she could talk to the dead, how another, unseen world was open to her... somehow.

"I feel his presence here, in this house." She let her eyes roam the room. "He loved it here, and I believe his spirit remains, along with his likeness."

She was speaking in riddles. "What do you mean, his likeness?" I sputtered.

"We had the best painter in the country come here and paint my grandfather," she said. "I was only a young child at the time, but I still remember the smell of the acrylics. My mother chided me not to get too close and distract my grandfather, but he was always kind. Always patient." She sounded faraway, like she was transported back in time.

"Your family had his portrait done," I reasoned, "and now it feels like his spirit is still here... because of that." My mind was clunking along. Could she mean that the spirit cabinet was here, in this house? Maybe near the painting of Matthew Getty? *Find Matthew, and you'll find what I need.* That's what the witch had said. Could it be that simple?

I locked eyes with Gracie, who had torn her gaze away from her phone for a moment. Her manner was unreadable, and her throat moved like she was gulping, but then she turned back and started typing again.

Oh my god. I could not have been more annoyed with her. I knew she loved her tech but *come on!*

"Does every Getty have their portrait painted?" I asked.

"Oh yes," Ms. Getty said. "It's tradition."

"And do you have all the paintings here in this house, hanging on the walls?" I leaned forward. I'd seen paintings on my way in, but no portraits.

Ms. Getty waved her napkin in Nana's direction. "You haven't told them much, have you, Clementine? They must be nearly teenagers. It really is time that they learn a thing or two."

I didn't know what she was talking about, and I wanted to ask more questions, find out where Matthew's painting was, but Nana looked like she was going to respond. She grabbed her notepad and started writing furiously. I held my breath and hoped Nana was able to keep her word about being nice.

After a minute, she slid her notepad across the table to Ms. Getty, who leaned over to read the message.

"I'm sorry to hear that the girls lost their father," she said, "and I'm sorry that this situation with the witch has you in a bind. It really is a shame." She slid the notepad back across the slick tabletop.

So Nana was being nice, but Ms. Getty wasn't.

Meanwhile Gracie kept texting. Didn't she care about what was happening? Didn't she want to help?

"You call it a shame," I said to Ms. Getty with new anger, "but it's more than a shame. It's our family. They're *frozen*. Please. We need your help. Could we just borrow the spirit cabinet? Maybe we could return it after?"

"Young lady," Ms. Getty said as she straightened in her chair, "do you know what would happen if I gave it to you?"

"I'm pretty sure my family would be saved."

She ignored me. "I'll tell you—unspeakable horrors would devastate all of Galveston. That witch had four items when she was banished: a candelabra, a tambourine, an accordion, and the cabinet in which she kept her things. The candelabra disappeared from this very house back in 1920, the year of the plague. An infuriating prig of a servant took it. My grandfather decided it would be safer to keep the witch's possessions in institutional settings, under their security. But the tambourine was pilfered from the Bryan Museum after it had been on display for just a few years. Vandals smashed the exhibit to bits before disappearing with the instrument. The accordion was housed at the Rosenburg Library for several decades, but it too was ripped from safekeeping by a thief who was never caught." Ms. Getty paused to shake her head, as if these thieves were the absolute scum of the earth.

"From what I've heard, those three items were eventually returned to the witch. Blackmail, you see. She freezes people's loved ones and makes innocent victims do her bidding, track them down. Like you." She nodded her head at me. "But if she gets all four... I'm telling you, horrors will rain down on this island. Maybe another hurricane. Maybe another plague. Maybe worse. Is that what you want?"

I couldn't think to say anything besides: "No."

She flung down her napkin as if I hadn't agreed with her. "The spirit cabinet was in the mayor's office for years—a gesture of goodwill toward the town, you understand, as we are one of Galveston's oldest families—but after so much recklessness with the other items, I had to change course. That cabinet isn't safe anywhere but here, under my own watchful care."

I was right! The spirit cabinet *was* here. In this house.

A plan started to form in my head.

"But maybe if we let the witch have all her things again," I started, "she'd be happy and she'd treat everyone better. Maybe there wouldn't be a hurricane or a natural disaster." I was full of it. First,

I was pretty sure the witch was irreversibly evil. And second, I was also pretty sure Ms. Getty would never agree to give up the cabinet.

I was starting to think of the situation like it was a soccer match: if you went straight for the goal, a player on the opposite team might come at you and steal the ball and you'd lose your chance. Sometimes the best course of action was to dribble to the outside or show off some fancy footwork, dodging back and forth, as you waited for the perfect shot. In other words: I had to buy more time until I figured out the rest of my plan.

Ms. Getty made a scoffing noise. "If that witch got her things back, chaos would come. Chaos!" She turned to gaze at Nana. "Speaking of chaos, what happened to the fence your people put up, Clementine? It doesn't do its job very well, does it? First your husband and now your granddaughter?"

Nana's face transformed into a half grimace, and I butted in. "It's fine. The fence is fine. I had to jump really high to get over it." Did I feel bad about this lie? Absolutely not. "Like I said before, I should have listened to my nana. She always told me not to go into that marsh. She said the witch was mean, but I didn't listen. I was… I was a bad kid," I said, finishing strong.

"Indeed, you were," Ms. Getty said. She looked pleased at that.

Fine. She could think what she wanted. Because the extra time had worked! A plan had occurred to me: I just had to get out of this room and find a way to see the rest of this house. I had to look for that painting!

I knew what to do.

"I think we can be on our way," I said, and I let my back curve as if I was submitting to her every whim, "but could I please use your restroom before we take off?"

"If only the young people would listen to us, right, Clementine?" Ms. Getty said this to Nana as if I hadn't spoken. "What's that saying about tossing pearls to swine?"

Nana didn't change her expression.

"Really," I said. "I'm so sorry, but I have to go real bad." I scooted my chair back and stood, and as I did, I heard a faint creaking sound. Like maybe Ms. Getty had a cat too. One as big as Tofu.

"Yes," Ms. Getty said, still ignoring my request, "you should have listened. You are a very bad child." She actually waggled a finger at me.

"Sure," I said. "I am and I should have. Absolutely. But, speaking of listening, I really have to pee." Gracie looked at me like I was being weird, which, I guess I was.

"Do you?" Ms. Getty questioned.

"Very badly." I bounced from one foot to the other, hoping to sell it.

Ms. Getty held up a hand like a school crossing guard. *Stop.* "So," she said, "you'd like me to think that you'll just use the restroom and then be on your way."

"Uh, what else would I do?"

She looked ready to pounce. "You may go," she said with a gesture toward the door that led to the foyer, "but my help will wait for you outside the bathroom door. They will listen to you pee—as you so bluntly put it—and then they will walk you back here." A tone of victory crept into her voice. "Is that what you want?"

She was onto me. Dang it, this woman was a predator through and through.

I sat.

"I didn't think so," Ms. Getty said, triumphant.

Nana wrote something on that notepad and slid it Ms. Getty's way.

"The past is the past, is it?" Ms. Getty leaned back in her chair.

Nana grabbed the notepad again and started scribbling.

I'd had enough. Abandoning all thoughts of being polite, I slammed my fists on the table. "Why? Why can't you just help us?"

"I could help you," Ms. Getty said in a manner so serene that it bordered on cruelty, "but chaos will come if I do. I must think about more than just your little family." I was about to say more, to really let her have it when she kept going. "Besides, my great-grandfather made the choice for me a long time ago. He chose to cut off your side of the family. We simply couldn't see eye to eye."

Wait. *My side of the family?* What did that mean?

Ms. Getty continued, "Percival Getty earned all the wealth you see here. He started investing in the railroads but then moved into agriculture and then later to the automobile industry. A brilliant mind," she said.

Nana let out a sigh like this woman was insufferable, which, I had to agree, she was.

"What do you mean *my* side of the family? And why are you talking about some rich guy from a long time ago?" I asked.

"I'm talking about him," she said, and she folded her hands and leaned toward me, "because he is important to this story. You see, he had three children: Matthew, Abigail, and Libby. He cut Libby out of the will after she married a dolt of a man. He saw that she wasn't worthy of a true investment, and he left her only a small bit of property on the other side of town, near the marsh."

"Well, I don't care." It came out of my mouth before I could stop it. "I don't care about your great-grandfather and who he cut out of his will. He sounds mean and you are too."

I heard a bump from another room in the house, and my mind again went to the thought that Ms. Getty must have a cat. I glanced up at the ceiling, the direction from which the sound had come, and then at Gracie, who'd also looked up. Gracie's eyes held something I couldn't read, but then dang it, she turned back to her phone and started texting again.

Ugh.

Nana and Ms. Getty didn't seem to have heard whatever bumped upstairs.

I took a breath. "Just let me borrow the spirit cabinet," I said, trying to sound forceful. "Please. I'll go and I'll do what I have to and then I'll return it and I won't ever bother you again."

Gracie jumped up from her chair, suddenly and inexplicably. "You're...you're a terrible woman," she yelled at Ms. Getty. She didn't sound mad, exactly—it was like she was acting—but as she went, her voice gained momentum and emotion. "We're here because we need your help and you! You want us to just go home?" Her eyes were wild. "We can't go home!" she screeched. "Not without that key to the mausoleum! We need it! We need it!"

What the...?

What was going on with her?

Had she not been listening this entire time?

I could have strangled her.

Nana wrote something on her notepad and pushed it Gracie's way, but Gracie didn't bother to look at it. She kept going, shouting at Ms. Getty, "We really, really need that key! Won't you please give it to us? We believe the spirit cabinet is in the mausoleum and we need to get inside!"

I glanced at Nana's notepad, where she'd written, *THE SPIRIT CABINET ISN'T THERE.*

At least Nana had been paying attention.

Gracie didn't stop. It was like someone had pressed an On button, triggering a version of Gracie I'd never seen before. She shouted, "I'm so mad! I'm so upset!" She pushed her chair out of the way and paced around the room, her arms waving wildly, one hand clutching her phone. She gave the screen the quickest glance before heading back to her spot at the table and scooping up her glass of water. "I'm so upset I just might throw this!" She gripped the glass in a menacing way.

Never in my life had I seen my calm, collected, and uber polite sister do anything like this. It was so unlike her, I had a fleeting moment of wondering if she had been possessed.

"Clementine," Ms. Getty said, "control your granddaughter, please, or I'll have to summon Patrick to escort you out immediately."

"I won't calm down!" Gracie shouted. "I'm so angry, I'm going to do it!"

And then she did. Holy crumbs! She threw the glass toward the far corner of the room. It hit the wall and bounced onto the rug. The water spilled everywhere, but the glass didn't break.

Ms. Getty gasped and stood up, hurrying to the intercom. She tapped the screen. "Patrick, Beatrice, I need you in the formal dining room. This instant!"

I gave Gracie a look like *Have you lost your mind?*

She looked back at me with urgency in her eyes. We didn't have a twin moment of reading each other's minds or anything, but somehow I figured out what she wanted. She needed me to help her make a big scene.

Weird... but this was Gracie—Gracie, who got As on all her assignments. Gracie, who had never overslept or been tardy in her life. Gracie, who had asked if she could take the STAAR test a second time because she thought it was fun.

Maybe she had a plan I couldn't yet fathom.

I grabbed my water glass. "Yeah, I'll throw mine too!" I squawked. "And I'll... I'll hit you right in the head with it!" Did this take it up a notch? Sure. I wasn't really going to do it, though. Not in a million years. I was angry and trying to help Gracie, but I knew right from wrong. I tossed my glass to the corner. It clinked against Gracie's.

Nana gasped, obviously horrified. She wrote and held up her notepad so both Gracie and I could see it. *STOP THIS NOW, GIRLS!*

But we didn't.

We kept at it. I scooped up anything I could find and threw it. Gracie made a bunch of noise, calling, "Ahhh-hhh!" It was a constant stream, a loud river flowing out of her mouth. I added to the cacophony, spouting "I'll throw this and that and that" as I chucked things into the corner. We were raising a real racket, and Ms. Getty shrieked into that intercom as if her life depended on it. "Come now! Patrick, Beatrice! Get to the formal dining room, this instant!"

Steps sounded and Patrick burst into the room a nanosecond later, holding his arms out like he was ready to tackle a six-foot villain. He took in the situation: Ms. Getty near the intercom, frantic. Gracie, her mouth open, yelling. Me, tossing stuff. (I was down to the napkins.) Nana standing, flashing that notepad, completely frazzled.

Beatrice dashed in right behind Patrick. "Should I call the police?" she asked.

Ms. Getty's breaths heaved out. "Get them out. Now!" She pointed at us as she screeched, "Go now or the cops will be on their way! We'll have you charged with criminal trespassing!"

Gracie glanced at her phone and stopped shouting. "Almost ready," she said, which was odd but clearly not the oddest thing that had happened today.

I knew I had to follow her lead. "Yeah, we're almost ready."

"You'll be going NOW," Ms. Getty said in a huff. "I didn't ask you to come here, and I certainly didn't ask you to... to do all this." She gestured at the messy room.

"Let's go," Patrick said.

"Okay," Gracie said. She tapped a quick message on her phone. "Got it." She said this, but she didn't move toward the door. Still following her lead, I held my ground.

"Go!" Ms. Getty ordered.

Nana leaned on the table like she was exhausted but now not just from this day and going all over town but also from having to deal with two extremely naughty children—near criminals. She wrote something on her notepad and showed it to Ms. Getty.

"I'm sure they are *not* normally well behaved," Ms. Getty answered. "I'll tell you: Percival made the right choice all those years ago."

She was talking about her great-grandfather again. Ugh.

Patrick made a motion like he wanted to herd us into the hall.

"I hope you know that you work for a terrible woman," Gracie said to him. "She has something that we need to save our family and she won't give it to us even though it's just a stupid key."

Gracie was still going on about the key? Wow, she was behind.

"Move," Patrick said, and he wrapped his massive hand around her arm.

Gracie wriggled out of his grip. "I'm going, I'm going." She marched herself out of the room.

"Yeah, me too," I said. I made it sound like it was my own decision, but I was still following Gracie's lead.

Nana came after me. In the hallway, she shook me off when I tried to take her arm. I could see irritation in her half frown, in her balled fists, in her tight, straight back. There was nothing to do but make sure she made it safely out and then close the door behind me. I wanted to tell her sorry, to let her know that I was doing it all for Gracie, but I kept my mouth shut.

Outside, Nana made her way down the porch stairs quickly—probably as quickly as she could go—gripping the railing. She didn't look back at us as she walked toward the car.

"What's up with her?" Gracie asked.

"I don't think she was happy with how we behaved."

"Fair enough," Gracie said, and she elbowed me. "But awesome job in there."

"What are you talking about?" I asked. "I still have no idea what that was about and I hope you had a good reason for doing whatever it was you were doing because here we are without the spirit cabinet and without a clue what to do next."

She winked at me. My sister actually winked at me. "Nana has the right idea," she said. "Let's get to the car."

Chapter Twenty-Three

Get to the car. Sure, Gracie's lost her mind and maybe ruined our chance of saving Mom and Duck and Tofu, but a ride in Nancy's mom's bumper-stickered clunker will be just the thing to turn this day around.

Nana stopped at the driveway to write a note, which she showed to Gracie as soon as she stepped off the stairs.

"Got it. I behaved badly. So sorry," Gracie said quickly. "But we've got to go. It'll all make sense soon."

Nana stamped her foot.

"No really," Gracie said. "We need to *go*."

Huh.

The car sputtered in an angry way, like it was hurrying us along too.

Nancy rolled down her window. "Oh my gosh, you guys, get in!"

"Okay, okay." I made sure Nana was seated and her door was shut. Then I squished in as quickly as I could, and Gracie clambered in after me. As soon as we were all in, Nancy's mom threw the car in reverse, and we sped backward down the driveway with a force that almost gave me whiplash. It was—in a word—unsafe. We didn't even have our seat belts clicked when the car peeled out onto Broadway Avenue J.

That's when I saw what was between Nancy's knees: a large rectangular object sat on the floor of the car, about three feet high and two feet wide; brown wood, highly polished.

I sucked in a breath. "Is that what I think it is?" I was almost too scared to say it, too nervous to even think it.

"The spirit cabinet!" Nancy said with a squeal. "We got it!"

"You? You? You?" I couldn't get my mind around this impossibility. "You stole it?"

"Thanks to you guys distracting her," Nancy said, leaning forward to throw Gracie a huge smile. "Nice job."

"Those noises," I said as I remembered. What I'd thought was Ms. Getty's cat. "That was you?"

"Me and Mom," Nancy said. "When Gracie texted me that she thought the spirit cabinet was inside the house, we had to try." Nancy was beaming. "We knew Ms. Getty would never give it to you willingly."

Nana's head whipped to the left to stare at Nancy's mom. My bet was that the right half of her face looked astonished, but I couldn't tell from this angle. Nancy's mom grinned and nodded slowly to Nana like she was proud of herself.

"You knew the spirit cabinet was in the house?" I said to Gracie. I was stunned. "What was all that stuff about the key and the mausoleum? Heck, even as we were leaving you were still begging for that key."

"Throwing her off our track," Gracie said.

Unbelievable... Wild. Awesome!

I never would have thought that Gracie had it in her. This day, it was... I didn't even know anymore.

I turned back to Nancy. "So you broke into the Getty Mansion?"

"Does it count as a break-in when you merely open the front door?" Nancy joked. "Ms. Getty must have thought she'd get rid of you quick. She didn't lock it and she didn't turn the deadbolt. She left the alarm off too. I guess she trusted Patrick and Beatrice to keep watch in the meantime."

"We wouldn't have been able to do it without Gracie's help," Nancy's mom said from the front seat. "Those two were onto us. There was one squeaky door, and they must have heard it because they came scurrying our way. Ms. Getty has them trained like guard dogs."

"We hid in the biggest bathtub I've ever seen." Nancy giggled.

I reached over Nancy and stroked the top of the spirit cabinet. It was real—and we had it. "But how did Gracie know to create a diversion?" I was still trying to piece everything together.

"I was keeping in touch with Nancy the whole time. I can text *and* listen, you know," Gracie said with a grin. "When Ms. Getty starting talking about Matthew's spirit being in the *house*, I knew the cabinet had to be there too."

Nancy chimed in, "Gracie texted me to say we should look for Matthew's portrait. It's amazing what you can find online about rich people's homes. There were photos of the house from a magazine article years ago, and we spotted the portrait in one of them. The caption said it was in the second-floor hallway." She shrugged like it was no big deal. "So we rushed upstairs."

"But then that creaky door...," Nancy's mom said from the driver's seat.

"That's why I had to... you know... with the glass of water and the *Ahhhhh*." Gracie made that hideous noise again, the one she wouldn't stop making inside.

My mouth hung open. "Wow. Just... wow."

"Whatever you did," Nancy's mom said, "it was brilliant. Patrick and Beatrice were off and running, and we had the second floor to ourselves."

"The spirit cabinet was right under the portrait. Not much of a secure hiding place, if you ask me," Nancy said.

"To think it's been there for decades...," Nancy's mom said. "I've been looking in all the wrong places."

"Our *whole family* has been looking in the wrong places," Nancy added.

"What do you mean?" I couldn't fathom why Nancy's whole family would be involved. Of course, I remembered her uncle and how he got the accordion, but why had they been looking for the spirit cabinet? The witch hadn't frozen any of their loved ones.

The car interrupted Nancy as she opened her mouth to respond, though. We were stopped at a red light, at the intersection where we would veer left to head toward the beach, toward home, and the car made an angry noise and then shuddered like it had a fever.

"Oh gosh," Nancy's mom said. "Sorry, folks. We're overheating." She hit some buttons and turned a few dials on the dashboard, and a blast of hot air pushed against us.

Not helpful, I thought to myself. It was extra hot in the back seat, since we were packed so close together, sardine-style. That spirit cabinet took up most of the space available.

"Come on, baby," Nancy's mom coaxed.

"Not again," Nancy said.

"Again?" Gracie asked with a squeak.

Nancy's mom rolled down the windows. "Sorry," she said. "Best I can do right now." And she turned up that dial even more. The fresh air coming in from the outside barely helped. It was after five, which meant we were facing both the hottest part of the day *and* heavy traffic.

She eased the car onto Seawall Boulevard, where the cars were already bumper to bumper.

And our car kept on shuddering.

Everyone stayed quiet, maybe from the tension. We were only about four miles from home, but they'd be a long four miles, filled with stoplights and stop signs and tourists jaywalking to get to or from the beach. Not ideal. I thought of Mom and Duck and Tofu... frozen... helpless.

Nancy's mom sighed as the car seemed to hiss. "Sorry, people, my dashboard just lit up like a Christmas tree. I'm pulling over."

"Head to the right," Nancy said, pointing to Gracie's side of the car, "in the plaza there, where it's shady."

The "plaza" was a strip mall with an ugly row of stores and restaurants, and a few oddball businesses thrown in. A dentist's office, a Cajun seafood restaurant, a kite store, a Speedy Mart, and an eyeglasses shop. The Rainforest Cafe, complete with a water ride and boatloads of tourists, dominated the lot down the road. Across the street, on the sidewalk that ran alongside the beach, was a statue memorializing all the people who died during the Big Storm. That was Galveston for you.

"We'll have to stop for a bit," Nancy's mom said as she parked the car carefully. "Shouldn't have left her running all that time."

"We might as well get out. It'll take ten to twenty minutes," Nancy said to Gracie and me, like she was explaining how car trouble worked.

We clambered out. At least we were in the shade and an ocean breeze was blowing.

"So...," Gracie said. She took a seat on the curb.

"So...," Nancy answered, sitting next to her.

I was too antsy to sit, and Nana leaned against the car, looking droopy.

Nancy's mom must have noticed, because she said, "I'll run to that Speedy Mart and grab us some waters."

"Should we get an Uber?" Gracie asked no one in particular after Nancy's mom had gone. Nana tucked her hands in her pockets and watched the pavement below her feet.

"Or we could scooter home," Gracie said.

Oh brother.

But I'll give her this: she was trying.

And it would have been a good idea if we hadn't left our scooters in the Strand. "That's a no go," I said.

Realization crossed her face. "Oh no, oh no! We have to go back. Now we'll definitely get parking tickets."

"No one's going to ticket us," I said, impatient.

"Mom's going to kill us," Gracie said. She put her head in her hands.

Nancy patted Gracie's arm. "It'll be okay."

"It won't!" Gracie was close to crying again. Ugh.

"Look," I said, "parking tickets don't matter. Nothing matters now but getting the spirit cabinet back. Because, quite frankly, if we don't do that, we won't *have* a mom to kill us. She'll be frozen and social services or someone will come and take us away."

My words—the force of my words—swirled around the lot, boomeranged back, and seemed to smack us in the faces. Right away, I wished I could take back what I said, or at least how I'd said it, and mumbled an apology.

"It won't be long," Nancy said to Gracie. "Try not to worry. The car just needs a break. Ten more minutes maybe. Tops."

Gracie put her head on her knees and sighed.

But at least she wasn't crying.

You couldn't see the beach from here, but you could hear the waves if you tried hard enough. And if you closed your eyes and tuned out the other sounds—cars braking, kids laughing, moms yelling, seagulls crying for French fries—there they were: *crash, crash, crash.*

I took in a salty breath. My mind was still hung up on something Nancy had said in the car.

"Wait. Why has your family been trying to find the spirit cabinet?" I asked.

"Well," Nancy started. "My family's been after it for a *really* long time." She looked back at the car, where it sat inside. "Next family gathering, we are going to have a lot of celebrating to do."

"But...why?" I repeated. I remembered that Nancy's uncle had said that he was looking for the last item belonging to the witch, but he had never said *why.*

"We're Keepers," Nancy said simply. "Mom and me and my whole family. It's our job."

"Keepers?" I repeated.

"Keepers of what?" Gracie asked, looking up from her lap.

"The Alligator Witch's True History," Nancy said gravely.

Chapter Twenty-Four

Nancy's mom came over, clutching five bottles of water. Just in time too, if you asked me. I had wiped my upper lip at least three times in the past two minutes, and even though I held my back to the beach so it could stay cool in the breeze, my shirt was sticking to it. It was a total sweat-fest.

After a big, cold, refreshing gulp, I turned back to Nancy. "Keepers of the Witch's True History... What is that?"

Nancy was chugging her own water, and her eyes bounced up to meet her mom's. She set the bottle down and said, "Sorry, but I told them."

Nancy's mom nodded her approval. "They should know. It's about time." Her voice was as serious as a math test. She turned to Nana. "Mrs. Parker, I don't want to disrespect your boundaries, but I feel like the girls need to hear this."

Nana nodded and moved her hand in a *go ahead* kind of wave. It looked to me like she was moving as little as possible, conserving her energy maybe. She must have been exhausted.

Nancy said, "So yeah. We're Keepers. Ms. Getty is a Keeper too. She's the Keeper of the Witch's Things. Her father was before her, and her grandfather, Matthew, was before him. It's passed down. A family tradition."

"A family *job*," her mom corrected.

Gracie and I locked eyes, and one thing was clear: neither of us had any idea what Nancy and her mom were talking about.

"I thought you worked at the historical society," I said to Nancy's mom.

"Maybe we should start from the beginning," Nancy's mom said. "There are three types of Keepers. Descending from Percival Getty's three children."

"Hey!" Gracie interjected. "Ms. Getty mentioned his kids. Libby, Matthew, and..."

"Abigail," Nancy finished the list for her.

"She made it sound like we were related to one of them," I said.

"You are," Nancy said.

"How do you know that?" I asked. This made no sense.

"I know because we are too," Nancy said, lifting one shoulder.

"Nana?" I asked. I wanted confirmation, or maybe some kind of reassurance that Nancy wasn't jumping on board some wacky train and dragging us along for a ride.

Nana got out her notebook, but it took her a million years to do it. She was moving really slowly. Finally, she held up a note that said, LIBBY WAS YOUR GREAT-GREAT-GREAT-GRANDMOTHER.

"Hold. The. Phone," Gracie said, looking shocked. She jumped up and turned to stare at Nancy. "If we're related to Libby, then you're...you're..."

"Yup," Nancy said. "I'm related to her too." She raised her bottle of water in a kind of toast. "Abigail was my great-great-great-grandmother. That would make Libby my great-great-great-grand aunt, I think."

Gracie spun on her heel and walked forward a few steps into the parking lot. She reasoned, "So that makes us... So we're related? You and me?" She looked back at Nancy.

"That's right," Nancy said. "Pretty distant cousins, but yeah."

"And that means," I spouted, "we're all related to Ms. Eloise Getty? Gross!" The thought made me want to throw myself on the pavement, but that would be a Mistake with a capital *M* because anything that had been sitting out in the sun all day would be burning hot.

"Wait," Gracie said. "We're related." She was still talking about her and Nancy, like she couldn't wrap her mind around it.

"We are," Nancy confirmed.

"You're my cousin."

"Yeah," Nancy said. "But like third or fourth or something like that. I'm not sure how it works when you go back that far."

"Hey," I said as I finished my water. "How come we aren't rich?"

"Percival Getty was not afraid to cut people out of his will," Nancy said.

"That's right!" Eloise Getty's comments came back to me. "Libby married someone he didn't like."

"Yes. He punished her, but he cut Abigail off completely. Libby at least got some land by the marsh," Nancy explained. "Abigail was shunned by the family. I'm talking, like, she was never allowed to set foot in her house again after what went down with the witch."

I was about to ask Nancy more, but Gracie cut me off, demanding: "How long have you known all this?" Her face was red, and it didn't look like it was from the heat—she only turned that color when she was angry. "You knew we were related." She pointed at Nancy. "You knew about Libby and Abigail and Percival . . . and you never told me?"

"Uh . . ." Nancy squirmed, still sitting on the curb. "I wasn't allowed to."

Gracie turned to face the car. "Nana?" she said. When Nana didn't respond, she cried, "Nana?" in a louder voice.

Nana watched her shoes and shook her head slowly, slowly.

Nancy's mom cleared her throat and said, "We didn't know how much you had been told. We didn't want to overstep."

"Nana?" Gracie cried again with even more urgency. "You knew Nancy was my best friend. Did you know that she was related to me?"

Nana finally wrote something on the notepad and flashed it to Gracie. *I SHOULD HAVE TOLD YOU.*

"Yeah," Gracie said, crossing her arms. "You should have."

NOT JUST ABOUT NANCY, Nana wrote. She turned to a clean page to finish her thought. *ALL OF IT.*

"All of what?" I asked.

"That you're Keepers too, of course," Nancy butted in. She stood up too and counted on her fingers as she spoke. "Ms. Getty's family is the Keepers of the Witch's Things, my family is the Keepers of the Witch's True History, and your family is the Keepers of the Marsh."

"Keepers of the Marsh?" I parroted back.

Nana nodded. She wrote, *OUR DUTY*, on her notepad. It made me think of Dad's note, the one I'd found in that drawer along with Dad's key. And I remembered that long story she'd written to me about Dad and the key to Papa's trunk. The handwriting! Nana must have written the note. She was the one talking about a duty.

"So we keep the marsh," I said. "Is that why Ms. Getty asked you about the fence?"

Nana nodded.

"Because we're supposed to keep people out of the marsh—it's our duty—but I clearly got through the fence to talk to the witch."

Nancy said, "That's not why the fence is there. Your great-great-grandmother, Libby Getty, wanted to keep the witch *inside* the marsh. She wanted her to remember that she was always watching her, guarding her, holding her in there."

I took this in. It didn't make sense. "A fence like that couldn't keep the witch inside even a little," I spouted. "She can fly."

"She can?" Nancy asked.

I nodded. "She could totally get out if she wanted."

"Hmm . . . ," Nancy said, and it sounded like she was trying to take in new information too. "I never knew that. But I suppose it doesn't matter."

"Doesn't matter?" I asked.

Nancy shrugged. "Maybe she decided to stay until she got her things back."

"The things that were taken," I said.

"Abigail Getty wrote a whole book about what happened in the year 1900," Nancy said. "She wrote down everything that Zofia went through, and, believe me, it wasn't good. Having her things taken was only part of it."

"Zofia," I said, "the witch?"

She nodded. "Zofia and Abigail Getty were friends, but the people from the town didn't understand her. They threatened to kill Zofia. After the Big Storm, they marched her down to your part of town; they held torches and knives and rifles. They threatened to burn her alive. They banished her to the marsh, and she went in, as willingly as one can under that kind of circumstance. Libby Getty vowed to keep her in the marsh. She had men with clubs and guns patrolling the marsh's perimeter for years and years."

"Why would she do that?" I asked.

A bunch of seagulls flew overhead, diving and cawing and fighting over a piece of food. One would get it, then another would steal it, then a third would swoop in. One prevailed, and the group soared away, headed for the beach.

"Zofia was a spiritualist," Nancy said. "She could speak to the dead, and lots of people in the town, including Libby Getty, thought that meant she was evil. They blamed her for the hurricane of 1900 and all the damage it caused."

"That's silly," Gracie said, scoffing. "Everyone knows Galveston is prone to bad weather; hurricanes hit all the time."

"Sure," Nancy said. "We know that now, but back then..."

"Could the witch really speak to the dead?" I pressed. I'd heard this too many times, but never with a definitive answer.

"I think so," Nancy said. "At least, that's what Abigail's book suggests."

Those seagulls came back and threatened more in-air hijinks but just as suddenly, they veered off to the right. Maybe some kids were coming out of the Rainforest Cafe with leftovers.

"So we're Keepers and you're a Keeper and you've known about this for a while." Gracie was talking to Nancy but not looking at her. She had her arms crossed tightly over her chest, and her face was still red. "Someone should have let us in on this... history or whatever it is."

Nana flashed that page again that said, *I SHOULD HAVE TOLD YOU.*

"When were you planning on it?" Gracie sounded angry at Nana too.

Nana sighed and wrote, *I WAS GOING TO... SOON.*

"*When?*" Gracie yelped.

Nana showed us the page again. It now read, *I WAS GOING TO . . . ~~SOON~~ BUT . . .*

"But what?" Gracie demanded.

"But she had a stroke," I said softly. "She couldn't."

THE FENCE, Nana wrote on a clean page. *YOUR MOTHER. IT WAS <u>HER</u> DUTY NOW.*

That jolted my mind back to Mom, Duck, and Tofu. *Right.* "We can argue about this all day," I said, "but it doesn't change anything. We need to get the spirit cabinet home. When will the car be ready?" I asked Nancy's mom. I wanted to be home, to be out of that strip mall and that angry conversation.

Frankly, it was weird seeing Gracie be mad at everyone. She was the calm one, the twin that held it together. I wasn't used to her like this. Part of me felt proud of myself—I wasn't getting mad—but the rest of me just wanted to be done with it.

"Let me give it a try," Nancy's mom said, getting into the car.

When she started the engine, it sounded normal. Thank goodness. She waved us toward the car, and I got Nana in and made sure her door was shut tight. That should have given Gracie plenty of time to climb in and sit in the middle, next to Nancy, but she didn't. She stood on the pavement looking mad, and gestured for me to get in the middle seat.

"Whatever," I said, sliding in. Gracie got in next to me and closed the door. "Let's just go. It's time to rescue our family from that evil witch's magic."

Next to me, Nancy clucked her tongue. "Zofia Kowalczyk was never evil. Just misunderstood."

Oh great. Dang it, I was just congratulating myself on being calm but now I was getting mad too.

"But she is evil," I argued. "She froze our mom and sister and cat!" My words seemed to bump around the car as Nancy's mom pulled us out of the strip mall parking lot. "Sorry," I said in a distinctly calmer voice, maybe trying to find my inner Gracie—the one that used to exist, the one who could remain calm in any situation. "You just... you should have seen her this morning. Her eyes were black and she got stretched out until she was way too tall, and she was kind of young but also old. She leaned over me and whispered in my face and her breath was so, so cold." I shuddered, even in the heat. "I'm telling you: she's evil through and through."

"She's angry," Nancy countered. "And rightfully so. Libby and Matthew took everything from her. Percival Getty tried to have her killed. Everyone in Galveston was looking for a scapegoat after the Big Storm. There was a witch hunt, and it ended with her in the marsh."

I remembered a picture I'd seen at Grandma LaSalle's—the one of a crying young woman being banished from the island, and this memory made a pit open in my stomach. Could it be true?

"It's painful to think about the role our town—our families—played in Zofia's transformation," Nancy's mom said gently. "But history matters."

"History mattered to our dad too," Gracie mumbled. "And he thought the witch was evil."

Everyone was quiet. We drove by the San Luis resort and then a miniature golf place and a few hotels. We passed by the area where the beach got rocky and people went crabbing. More red lights. Businesses became sparser as we moved farther south, toward our house, toward the marsh. The houses in this part of the island were big and pastel colored. Beside me, Gracie huffed, still mad. Nana was quiet, and Nancy looked sullen.

I swallowed down a bad feeling. We had the spirit cabinet, but everything was terrible. I was confused—and nervous to go back and see that witch. Nothing felt right.

I only knew one thing for sure: this was my fault.

I had to save Mom and Duck and Tofu.

I had a job to do. A duty.

Chapter Twenty-Five

Nancy lifted the spirit cabinet and carried it with what looked like reverence. She set it on the driveway between us. We had arrived, at long last. We were home.

"I have to take it to the witch," I said, just in case Nancy or her mom had any funny ideas. Their family had been looking for it for a long time, after all.

"We know," Nancy said. She patted the top of the cabinet.

"Your family doesn't want it?" I asked, suspicious.

"We just want Zofia to have her things back," she said.

"Lana, should I come with you?" Gracie asked.

I wondered if she was saying that to get away from Nancy. But at the end of the day, it didn't matter why she was asking. My answer would be the same in any case. "I have to do this myself." I glanced at the marsh. "I went in there by myself this morning and I have to go back alone." I nodded at Nana, who had gotten out of the car and was looking shaky. "Besides," I said to Gracie, "you should get Nana inside and make her a cup of tea. You guys can be there when Mom and Duck and Tofu get unfrozen." I added darkly, "If everything goes right."

Nancy patted my shoulder. "It will. You'll see. Zofia is good at heart."

I didn't respond, but the look I gave her must have been grim because she added, "It'll be okay."

Gracie sighed. She said to Nancy, "I can't believe you knew all about this and never told me."

"I'm sorry," Nancy said.

I wanted to help Gracie, who still looked miserable, but I wasn't sure how and besides, I had to go.

"Be honest," Gracie said. "Were you friends with me because of all this Keeper stuff?"

Nancy rubbed the toe of her shoe on the driveway. "No...no! We've been friends since we were little! When Mom told me about being a Keeper, it was *so hard* not to tell you. But she made me promise." She looked at Nana for a moment. "She wanted you to hear from your family first. Like I said, it's a family thing."

"A family's *job*," Nancy's mom corrected her again.

"A duty," Nancy amended.

Gracie frowned.

"Really," Nancy said. "I wanted to tell you."

Gracie's shoulders were hunched forward. Her frown deepened and she turned to look away. Was she giving Nancy the silent treatment?

I had no patience for this.

"Listen," I said to them. "You two are friends. The truest of true friends. You worked together today. You tried to break into a mausoleum. You coordinated a home invasion. You understand each other. And you like each other. And you're really just...perfect." They had to see it, right? "So, work it out. Be friends again, okay? I have to go." The spirit cabinet was bigger than I expected and awkward in my arms.

"Good luck," Gracie said.

As I walked into our backyard, Gracie and Nancy kept talking but their words lost the harsh tones and dangerous points and the overall sound of misery. When the dead grass turned into dirt before it would again change to mud, I paused and glanced back. They were hugging.

Finally.

One crisis over. One more to try to fix.

The marsh was as hot as ever, and the AC from the car felt like a distant memory. I swatted a mosquito away from my ear. Still bug central. Sweat gathered on my face and across my back and under my arms as I made my way toward the stand of trees.

When I was a few feet away, the bugs stopped swarming. The crickets stopped chirping. The cicadas quit buzzing. The marsh seemed dead here. Fear swirled around my chest. What if the witch wasn't satisfied with this cabinet? What if she double-crossed me and kept Mom and Duck and Tofu frozen?

There was nothing to do but try. Nancy's words echoed in my brain: *Zofia Kowalczyk was never evil. Just misunderstood.* I hoped she was right.

"Hello?" I squeaked out. I cleared my throat and said, "I would like to talk to you, please."

Scratch! Screech! Scrape!

The limbs of the trees moved and changed and tangled in new ways. Then, a house stood in front of me, high up on alligator legs. Stairs unfurled to the ground. The witch appeared in the front door, at the top of the stairs. Her eyes were black voids, and she was stretched out—far, far too tall.

"Miss Kowalczyk," I said, trying to be polite. "Hello."

She jerked as if surprised I knew her name.

I held out her spirit cabinet, my arms aching. "I have this for you." I placed it on the driest piece of ground I could find and backed up a few steps. She flew down, out of her house, her ragged dress billowing out around her, and landed several feet from me. She looked nervous, I thought, or maybe weary. Like *she* suspected *me* of double-crossing.

"I'm sorry it's taken so long to return this to you."

She took a step toward me, and I tried to steel myself. What if she decided to go all *Hansel and Gretel* and eat me?

With a gulp, I tried to remind myself of Nancy's story. "I know the townspeople of Galveston let you down before," I began carefully. "I won't. I'm giving this back to you... forever. One of Abigail Getty's descendants helped me retrieve it."

The witch's body shortened—shrinking by about a foot—and she made a noise that sounded like sadness, like maybe hearing Abigail's name brought up something she hadn't felt in a long time.

"For the record," I said, "I'm sorry."

She took another step closer to the cabinet. Her body shortened again. "Oh," she said. Her voice sounded different. More human. She knelt by the spirit cabinet and touched it, like she couldn't believe it was real. As she looked over it, her irises began shifting from black to a light brown.

This was working.

"I'm sorry for how they treated you," I continued. "What they did was not okay." My words sounded silly, trite, but they were true. "I hope getting this back makes you feel better."

She still knelt by that old wooden piece of furniture, and her hands moved over it like it was the most precious thing in the world. "Thank you for bringing me this," she said softly.

"Um, no problem," I said even though it had been a bit of a problem—a very, very big problem.

She straightened up and said, "Spirits, come," and she held her hands high in the air. Instruments banged and shook. The tambourine, accordion, and candelabra flew out of the open door of her house and moved to hover in the air above her. She opened the cabinet and smiled back at them. She said, "Here is your home." The instruments flew into the cabinet and glided onto the shelves inside. The candelabra stayed in the air, though. It wiggled at her like it was trying to talk. "Yes," she said to it. "You're right. There is work to do before you can rest." She made a flourish in the air with her hands, and called out, "Spirits, return."

A cold wind rushed past me, pushing against my back. The witch raised her head and held her eyes on the horizon, as though she was watching something over my shoulder. When she nodded and held out her hand in a gesture of welcoming something, I turned. Three lights, three flames were soaring through the air. They were headed toward us.

My heart jumped. "Are they okay now?" I meant Mom and Duck and Tofu. "I'm sorry," I added. "I didn't mean to be disrespectful. I know you haven't had your things for a long time... I just really need my mom and little sister and cat back." The lights floated past me and came to the witch. They hovered in the air. "Please," I said. Tears climbed into my eyes, making my vision watery. "I need my family."

"Rest now," she said. But she wasn't talking to me. The flames settled on top of the candlesticks in the candelabra, looking like normal flames. "Your job is done." She blew out the candles. "You may return home now too," she said to the candelabra. It fluttered into the spirit cabinet and landed on a shelf next to the instruments.

As the cabinet closed its doors, the witch stood tall, her hands clasped by her chest. "Now there's only the problem of me," she said.

I didn't know what to say to that. I didn't know what she meant.

She again lifted her arms, more gracefully this time. A wind swirled—a warm breeze. Tall grass uprooted and spun around her. Droplets of marsh water joined in the whirlwind. It looked like a magical, miniature tornado. It lasted a minute, and when everything settled back to the earth and the wind blew itself out, the witch stood in front of me, barely recognizable. She was a normal size, and her eyes shone brightly. Her clothing was mended—the fancy red dress with black trim again—and her face was beautiful, no traces of anger or age. She was a young woman, not much older than me.

She stepped toward me, but I didn't flinch. This was not the Alligator Witch. I could see that Nancy had been right—Zofia Kowalczyk was just a girl who'd been mistreated and misunderstood.

"Thank you," she said. She looked at me for a long moment, like she was studying me. "You came here to ask about someone who passed. Someone close to you?"

"My dad," I said. "He died a few years ago and I really miss him." It might have been the stress of the situation or misplaced adrenaline or just a bunch of heightened emotions all crashing down on me at once—but I couldn't hold back the tears any longer. This time they were sad tears. For Dad. "I just wish I knew if he was okay. If he, if he is still... somewhere."

Zofia closed her eyes and lifted her chin. It looked like she was listening for something. Or listening to someone. When she opened them again, she said, "Your dad *loved* history." She smiled.

"Y-yes, he did," I said. Was she for real?

She closed her eyes again and seemed to be listening, still...

longer this time. She nodded along, like someone was talking to her and then she said, "He wants you to know that the house you visited today was made of limestone and brick. It was constructed between 1893 and 1895. It features hand-carved wood, stained glass, coffered ceilings, and many family heirlooms." She gave a short laugh, which sounded like bells.

"He says he always wanted to go inside, but the woman that lives there is not nice. She thinks about history in a different way than he does. History to him is a set of questions to be asked, lessons to be learned, insights to be gained. But to her, it is power." She opened her eyes and stared directly at me when she said, "He says he loves you very much. He wishes he could give you a hug, even if you wiggled away."

Dad always was a hugger and I ... well, I wasn't. I'd say, *Enough, Dad*, until he let me go. Now, all I wanted to do was to crawl into his arms. Another dang tear rolled down my face.

Part of me wanted her to keep talking, keep telling me what Dad said. But I knew Zofia was done here. Done with Galveston. It was time to let her go. "Thank you," I whispered. "Thank you, Zofia."

She nodded at me and turned to face her house. "Are you ready, my friend?" she asked, and the house seemed to breathe. It moved in a way that reminded me of a chest rising and falling, and then it growled. Not in a mean-dog way, more like the sound a pet would make when it was happy. "Let's be on our way," she said.

The house swirled and creaked, and the branches twisted, and, in a moment, it was a bunch of dead trees and some old wood with an alligator standing guard near it.

Zofia—I couldn't think of her as a witch anymore—walked to the alligator, bent down, and patted its snout. "Thank you for our time together." She turned to me. "Goodbye, girl of the town. Please give Abigail's relatives my regards."

"I will."

Zofia and the alligator stood close together, and something started pouring out of their bodies. It looked like smoke, or maybe a bazillion gnats? There were two balls of them, swirling and moving. They came together to form one bigger black ball, and then they shot up into the air super fast. Gone.

When I looked back at Zofia and the alligator, they were both wrinkly and old-looking. The color drained from their clothes and skin. As I watched, open-mouthed, they turned even grayer, disintegrating, cracking into pieces and then collapsing into piles of dust.

"What the—?" I said out loud. It was horrifying.

And then there was nothing. Just the ground, and the grass, and the salty, decaying smell of the water.

A mosquito landed on my face close to my ear and hummed. I swatted at it. The cicadas buzzed. The bugs were back. A bird squawked from a tuft of grass nearby. The marsh was alive again.

The spirit cabinet was sitting on the ground where I'd put it. "Hey, you forgot—" I started, but I stopped myself. She was gone.

Maybe she meant for me to keep it.

No—not me. I knew who should have it.

I picked up the cabinet and started for home.

Chapter Twenty-Six

Outside the front door, I held my breath. I pressed my ear to the wood. I could make out the soft sound of murmurs. People talking. That must be good news. More tears spread to my eyes—this time, happy ones. I couldn't wait to see my family.

I turned the knob, but the door wouldn't open. It jammed after a few inches, as if something was lying against it.

Or someone.

Or some cat!

Tofu. Was he okay? Was he still frozen? Fear gripped me. Maybe my ears were playing tricks on me. Maybe it was only Gracie and Nana talking, and nothing had been set right.

But then the door opened and when I moved inside, Tofu was strutting away, his kitty tail curved in the air like a question mark.

"Tofu!" I shouted. He turned, crouched, and looked startled. When he saw it was me, he turned again in that I-don't-care kind of way only cats can and kept walking.

I placed Zofia's cabinet on the floor, tugged off my muddy shoes, and went after Tofu as quickly as I could without frightening him again. "I'm so glad you're okay," I told him. I scratched him near the ears the way he liked. "Don't ever let me do something that stupid again, okay?"

He blinked at me like I was on my own before padding off.

I wanted to chase after him and scoop him up and hug him tight, but Mom's voice was coming from the kitchen, and I couldn't stay away from her one second more. As much as I loved Tofu, I loved my mom more and I needed to see her now, now, now! I sprinted through the house. "Mom!"

Mom and Duck and Nana and Gracie were in the kitchen. I ran over and practically jumped on Mom, who was sitting at the table. "You're not frozen!"

"Whoa, whoa," she said, and she hugged me back. "I'm okay." She laughed like everything was fine, like she'd been okay the whole time. "Y'all keep saying I was hurt, or frozen, or whatever, but I wasn't, I swear. I was fine. I *am* fine." She pulled me away to look me in the eyes. "Everything's fine now." She lowered her voice to whisper, "I just don't know how it got to be this late in the day."

Nana sat nearby, a cup of tea in front of her—probably Gracie's doing. She looked better than she had since the cemetery. More energized. Gracie must have put a *bunch* of sugar in. She wrote in her notebook, *THAT'S WHAT HAPPENS. FEELS LIKE WAKING UP ONLY TO FIND TIME HAS PASSED.*

Duck sat on the other side of Gracie, but she wasn't interested in the conversation. She gripped her Nintendo Switch, which she hammered at with all her ten-year-old might. "Die! Die! Die!" she said to some monster on the screen.

I still wasn't a fan of that word, but I wasn't going to let it bother me now. I ran over to her. "Duck!" I cried, and I tried to hug her, but she didn't hug me back. She was busy.

"Sorry," I said to her, and I tugged her ponytail.

"I didn't get to play all day and now it's almost bedtime. No fair." She glanced at me. "I'll get over it. I guess." She had an edge in her voice, a mischievous one. She wasn't really mad at me, only playing at it. "Thanks for unfreezing me."

"Sorry I got you frozen in the first place," I said.

"Well, I don't know about the rest of you," Mom said, standing, "but I'm starving. Kind of like I haven't eaten all day." She gave a small laugh. "How's pasta sound? I think there's some sauce in the pantry."

"I'll get it," I offered. I was hungry too. Famished.

After I handed the jar to Mom and she put some water on to boil, Gracie asked, "So what happened, Lana? Did you see her? Did you...?"

"I did," I said, and then I hesitated, because how do you even talk about what happened out there? Had I watched Zofia and the alligator die? Maybe. I didn't know. But I had to set the record straight about one thing. "She...wasn't evil. Just like Nancy said. She was misunderstood. She and her alligator are gone now."

"Gone?" Gracie asked.

"Yeah."

"Huh," Mom said with a shrug. "Galveston without a witch doesn't seem possible."

Duck sang, "Alligator Witch in the marshy trees, nasty, nasty mean old witch is she. Die, witchy-witchy, die, witchy-witchy. Please just let us be."

"I'll give you twenty bucks to never sing that song again, Duck," I said, and Duck cocked her head.

"Okay," she said agreeably.

I knew all the kids her age sang it, but *we* shouldn't. Since we knew the truth now. Since we knew Zofia wasn't really a witch.

Nana wrote in her notepad, *THAT WITCH IS EVIL!*

"No, Nana," I said with as much kindness as I could.

Duck gave me a side-eye. "She did freeze me."

"I know," I acknowledged, "but I don't think she meant to... or, I don't think she would have if she hadn't been scared and hurt."

Nana made a grunting noise.

"I know it might take some time, Nana, but please believe me. She wasn't evil."

Instead of responding, Nana took up her cup of tea, blew on it, and sipped.

Good enough.

I vowed to keep working on her. Nana and her family had believed in the story of the Alligator Witch for generations. It would take some time to set things right.

———•———

Mom served everyone heaping piles of pasta with sauce.

It was nice to be together and eating...

But there was something else that had to happen. Something I had to do.

"Mom," I said, "I'd like to talk about Dad."

She wiped her mouth with her napkin and kept her eyes on the cloth. As if she didn't want to look at me.

"Dad isn't here with us, but he was a part of all we did today," I said. I wound the key out from under my shirt. "He was the reason I bothered that—" I almost said *witch*, but I stopped myself in time. "He was the reason I went into the marsh this morning in the first place," I corrected. "And I miss him. I need to talk about him. Sometimes. Maybe a lot. I'm tired of pretending that he never existed."

WE ALL MISS HIM, Nana wrote.

Yes, she was willing to talk... or communicate, somehow, at any rate. She'd be my way in. "You shared a lot about Dad with me today," I said to Nana. "You told me things I never knew. And,

Gracie, you talked about him today too. You pointed out how he would have loved all the old stuff we saw."

"He would have," she said quietly. Tears puddled in her eyes and her face got red, but her tears didn't annoy me, not even a little. I understood them. Heck, I'd cried today too.

"He really would have liked that presentation at the historical society," I said, "even though it was so boring."

Gracie hiccupped.

Mom was still silent, and I knew if I didn't reach her now, it wouldn't happen.

"What's something you remember about him, Mom?"

She wiped her mouth with that napkin again and said, "Lana. Not tonight. It's been a hard day."

It had been a hard day, but these feelings had been balled up inside me for too long. I had to do this.

"Please, Mom," I pushed. He felt so close to me now, and I didn't want that to go away. I needed to talk about him and remember him, and it felt like I needed that as much as I needed to breathe.

Mom stared at the table. She wasn't budging. "Do you remember that night we went to Spaghetti Warehouse and Dad ordered an entire cheesecake? The waitress was like, 'Sir, we can't do that,' and he said, 'Sure you can.' And then he spoke to the manager, and they brought it out?"

"I remember that!" Gracie spouted.

"We didn't eat it all," I said. "We barely got through half, but it was awesome."

Gracie smiled. "I was shaking from all the sugar after downing two pieces and Duck had it all over her face. She kept saying, 'More, more! More, Daddy.'"

I let out a laugh.

Duck's frown grew deeper. "I don't remember."

"It was a long time ago," I said as a kind of apology. "You were still in a high chair back then."

"And so jacked up by the time the bill came that you were kicking and screaming and Dad had to carry you out to the car," Gracie said. "Maybe it's better that you don't remember it."

"But I want to!" Duck said, and she started crying. "I want to remember Daddy too."

I laid a hand on her shoulder. "We can help you, Duck." She was only eight years old when he died. "Right, Mom?"

Mom's throat moved like she was swallowing something painful.

I kept going. "How about a different memory? How about when he gave me that piggyback ride at the Houston Zoo? It had rained so hard, I lost my flip-flop in that big puddle."

Mom's face was squished up tight.

"He carried you everywhere that day," Gracie said, adding to the story.

"His back must have killed him by the time we were going home." I smiled.

"No fair," Duck said. "I wish Daddy had given me a piggyback."

"He picked you up so you could see the elephants," I said.

"And the zebras and the red pandas," Gracie said.

"Come on, Mom," I said in a quiet voice. "I'm sure you remember. Better than any of us, I bet."

She just stared at the table.

I needed more. I pushed back my chair and ran into my room, where I had a picture from that day at the Houston Zoo. We were all soaked because of how much it had rained and, trust me, the Houston Zoo was not set up for pouring rain. In the photo, I had on only one flip-flop, but I looked happy. Dad kept saying, "It's just a little rain." He wouldn't call it a day even after the flip-flop had long disappeared. He wanted us to visit every exhibit, so we saw all the animals and got soaked. It was a happy trip—if a soggy one.

I brought the photo to the kitchen table and slid it under Mom's gaze before sitting back down.

"Duck, you had that little froggy hat that you used to love, and Gracie's pizza got rained on. And Dad...," I said. "What else did he do that day?" I waited for Mom to say something. For her to add to the story.

Mom wiped her hand across her nose and cheeks. She didn't answer.

Gracie said, "He liked watching the seals. We couldn't drag him away from their tank."

"They were splashing in the rain," I said.

"Wait! I remember that!" Duck said. She sounded excited. "One of them got that ring on his nose. Daddy laughed. He thought that was funny."

"Because it was!" I said, and I let out a chuckle. "That's where you got Snowy."

"That's where I got Snowy?" she asked.

"Yup. You begged Dad for a stuffed animal, and he couldn't refuse. I mean, he said no a million times, but you kept asking until he gave in."

Duck jumped out of her seat and ran off. Two seconds later, she was back, hugging her stuffed white leopard. "I had forgotten the story of how I got Snowy." She was crying.

Mom sniffled loudly. She reached over and pulled Duck in for a hug.

"Come on, Mom," I said. "Tell us what you remember."

She separated from Duck enough to look her in the eyes. "I thought you had enough stuffed animals. But your dad... he said, 'She's our baby.'" Mom gave another big sniff. "I said, 'Oh, come on.' 'No,' he insisted. 'She's our last baby.' And he made this sad face at me, and I totally gave in." Her voice cracked.

Duck squeezed Snowy to her chest. "Thanks, Mom."

I think Duck meant thanks for giving in and buying her the toy, but when I said, "Thanks, Mom," I meant for talking, for sharing what she remembered.

Mom let out a watery chuckle. "And he wanted me to crawl through those tunnels in the building with the fish, even though they're meant for kids."

"No way you were doing that," Gracie said. "Or me." She fake shivered. "Too many sharks."

"I should have done it," Mom said, and she put her hand over her mouth. "Your dad really knew how to live. He knew how to have fun." And then she was crying too.

"He was always doing goofy things," Gracie said. Tears ran down her blotchy cheeks.

"He gave the best hugs," Duck said. "I remember that."

"He did," Mom agreed, squeezing Duck. "You're remembering that right."

Nana held out her hand and I gave her the photo. She rubbed a fingertip over Dad's image and made a sound that was full of love.

I stood to give her a hug. "Thanks, Nana."

I looked over at Gracie. Her face was red, and her eyes were red, and she didn't look like she would stop crying anytime soon. They were all crying, and you know what? I was too. Again! And that was okay.

I had plenty of complaints about being a twin.

But here was the cool part: you got to experience life with someone. That person was always by your side.

Gracie and I had been through hard things together. In life, in the two years since Dad had died, and especially today. We had found our mom and our sister and our cat frozen, and we'd had to deal with it. And somehow along the way, we had become SISTERS. Yes, all caps.

In that moment, I understood our differences. I grieved by remembering. I grieved by wanting to talk about Dad and trying to keep him alive forever. But Gracie grieved by, literally, grieving. She was sad. It could not have been any simpler. It was just sad. There was no way around it. Dad was gone forever.

And in one of those rare twin moments, I mirrored my sister. My face was scrunched up. So was hers. My face was wet. So was hers. We were both crying. I went to her and cried with her. I hugged her and she hugged me, and we cried harder because some things never fully heal. Talking about Dad helped, but I was sad. So was Gracie.

Now we were sad together. We could be sad together.

We were sisters. We were twins. Fraternal, sure, but still twins.

I set the picture of us in Houston in the middle of the table, and we talked about Dad all through dinner. It was amazing and sad and wonderful and heart-wrenching. But good. Overall, it was good. I needed to talk about him. I missed him. And so did everyone else. We were sad, but we were a family, and we could talk about it. We could be together again. We could move on.

Zofia Kowalczyk helped us accomplish that.

Later that night, I knocked on Gracie's door. When she told me I could come in, I pushed it open. She was on her bed, phone in hand.

"Hey," I said, "um, I know this is going to sound strange or stupid, but thanks for everything."

"What are you talking about?" she asked.

"Everything. You know, today."

"I didn't do anything special," Gracie said.

"What?" Was she being for real? "Yes, you did. First off, you agreed to help me. You didn't yell or cry or even get too upset. You just got down to business. You went to the LaSalles' with me, and you were the first one on the lawn at Stoney Brook, and you knew where the storage unit was and at Ms. Getty's—don't even get me started about what you did there."

She let out a low chuckle. "I did successfully act like I had lost my marbles."

"You did more than that," I said. "You went out of your comfort zone. You pretended to be mad and then you threw your glass. You even raised your voice!" I let out a pretend gasp. "At an old person." I ended on a serious note: "I couldn't have done it without you."

Who would have guessed? My twin sister and I made a good team.

Gracie lifted one shoulder and brushed her perfect dark hair out of her pretty dark eyes. "I'm glad it all worked out."

"You did a kick-butt job," I said.

Duck had been walking in the hall near the open door and she stopped. "Mom!" she called out. "Lana's swearing."

"Kick-butt isn't a swear," I said with a laugh.

"Kind of close," Mom said from down the hall.

"I was talking about Gracie," I called.

"Oh, well, that changes everything," Mom said. "Gracie *is* totally kick-butt."

"MOM!" Duck said, sounding horrified.

"Time for bed," Mom said to Duck. "But, for the record, so are you." She pulled Duck into a hug. "Totally kick-butt." She glanced my way. "You too."

"Thanks, Mom."

As Mom got Duck into the bathroom to brush her teeth, I turned back to Gracie. "I guess I just wanted to say thanks."

"Thanks to you too," Gracie said. "This day... it ended up being pretty special."

"It did," I said with something like a sigh. I'd saved my family and gotten them to talk about Dad and now instead of being Keepers of the Marsh, we'd be something else. More like Nancy's family. "It really did," I said, and I didn't even flinch when, after I'd shut Gracie's door, I heard *Bump, bump, bump, ba-bump, ba-bump, ba-bump,* the pulsating sound of K-pop, echoing down the hall.

―・―

The next day, Gracie and Nancy got together. I tagged along... with a particular piece of furniture.

When I set it on the rug in Nancy's living room, she let out a quick, "Oh," and then, "Wow."

"I think Zofia wanted you to have it," I said.

Nancy moved to the spirit cabinet and rubbed the top of it in a way that reminded me of how Zofia had. She gently opened the doors. "The instruments," she said, "and the candelabra."

"Don't freeze anyone," I joked.

"You know," she said, straightening, "I might actually try my hand at spiritualism."

"Yeah, right," Gracie said.

"No, seriously," Nancy averred. "You never know. Maybe you can actually talk to the dead."

I didn't say anything to that, and I never told anyone about what happened out in that marsh—with Zofia communicating with Dad. It was my secret.

"Do you really think so?" Gracie asked, skeptical.

Nancy only raised a shoulder. "Lots of people swore it was true."

"I think you should try it," I said. When Gracie stared at me, I only shrugged. "Like Nancy said, you never know."

Chapter Twenty-Seven

That night, I dreamed about the Alligator Witch. We stood on the beach together. Her hair was in a neat bun and her dress—red with black trim—blew in the ocean breeze. She looked at me with kind eyes, and in that soft voice, she said, "Are you ready, Lana?" She smiled a ghost of a smile at me before reaching out. I took her hand in mine. One, two, three, we leaped up and up and up and flew into the air.

Together.

Acknowledgments

Thank you, first, to my agent, Rena Rossner. I feel so lucky to have her in my life and this book would not be in the world without her.

Thank you also to the team at Holiday House. Most significantly, thank you to Sally Morgridge, my amazing editor. She took this book to a whole new level. Her guidance and insight are irreplaceable. She is patient and kind, and all any writer could want. Thank you also to Chelsea Hunter, the designer; Vanessa Morales, the cover artist; Hayley Jozwiak, the copy editor; Veronica Ambrose, the proofreader; Mary Cash, the editor in chief at Holiday House; and Laura Kincaid, Sally's assistant editor.

I would never have made it this far in my writing career without my critique partners. Thank you to Jen Griswell, Michelle A. Barry, Tracy Townsend, Jen Griswell, Julie Dugger, and David Bridge.

This book is a love letter of sorts.

To Galveston, which I first visited in 2021. I caught fish; I ate seafood; I walked through the marsh (the Galveston Island State Park). There was a curious stand of trees—no witch I presume, but it seemed like there should be—and, if the warning signs were to be believed, plenty of alligators.

To my father, Phil, who passed away in July 2020. He didn't die from a virus like so many others that year, but Covid kept me from being at his side at the end.

To my mother-in-law, Carol, whose strategy for playing "One Night Ultimate Werewolf" is noted in the text. "Rarr!" Every time.

To my mom, Nancy, who is much like her namesake in the book;

always eager to help, she would have a pencil out and ready for you before you could even say, "Now where did mine go?"

To my fraternal twin sister, Michele.

To my brother, Matthew, who is sweeter and kinder than the Matthew in the text.

To David, my husband, who loves history and Galveston as much as I do, and who introduced me to Erik Larson's *Isaac's Storm: A Man, A Time, and the Deadliest Hurricane in History.*

To Felicity, my daughter, who likes mac and cheese as much as Duck does.

To Gabby, my daughter, who likes all things scary and who used to passionately fight hordes of endermen.

To my cat, Shiloh, who looks and acts an awful lot like Tofu.

To my graduate school education, which gave me an interest in the nineteenth century and introduced me to spiritualism.

Thank you to all those who have supported me along the way, to the #WritingCommunity on X (formerly Twitter), to Rena's Renegades, to my Baylor students who inspire me. Thank you to Chris Baron, Ally Malinenko, Dana Kramaroff, Madelyn Rosenberg, Heather Dean Brewer, Ben Guterson, Emily Bleeker, and Mark Olsen.